TIME WAITS FOR NO ONE

TIME WAITS
for
NO ONE

Diego Kent

LUMINARE PRESS
WWW.LUMINAREPRESS.COM

Printed in the United States of America

Luminare Press
442 Charnelton St.
Eugene, OR 97401
www.luminarepress.com

LCCN: 2024910612
ISBN: 979-8-88679-581-3

For Jeanine Basinger

CHAPTER 1

Certain work flows better after hours, way after hours. No meetings to attend, and the phones stop ringing. Delving deep into my staff's research, I can add notes to findings or request further details. Without interruptions, I'm more focused in drafting messages to outside contacts. Later, I sign off on correspondence, scribbled postscripts conveying more than words.

Today that solitary work lifts my spirits and frees me enough to indulge in running a lap around the mall before going home. Exposed patches of dirt dot the grass like merit badges, insignias of marches, protests, and celebrations past, including inaugurations.

I pause at the Lincoln Memorial to dwell on some of the president's words inscribed inside. This time of night, with no tourists or rangers around, serenity eases past solemnity. Leaving to complete a circuit, notions of purpose speed my pace.

At home in bed, I conjure a scene from a movie where a lion stalks the statue of Lincoln in the memorial. But I can't recall the name of the picture before falling asleep.

THE HOSPITAL advises me to walk the sick woman to the ER from the shelter. Given the snowstorm, waiting for an available ambulance might take an hour. It's only two blocks. We are skidding and sliding in six inches of snow. She tells me it hurts to breathe. She wraps her arms around my neck and says she can't walk. I lift and cradle her in my arms and continue. Wind is blowing snow in my face, and I can't wipe it away. I turn a corner and see the lights of the ER. The woman slips from my hands into the snow. I gather her up a wheelchair ramp and ring a doorbell. Libbie, in green scrubs, comes out through a glass door and joins us on the ground in a snow drift. She takes the woman's feet, and I lift under her arms. Libbie is calm as we struggle to bring the woman indoors. But the hospital is no longer there. Looking down at the woman, I see Libbie lying under the snow, only her face visible, her eyes bright. Snow continues to fall as I flail at the drift.

Defeated, I wake up, yet grateful for having spent time with Libbie.

AT THE office, I interrupt packing research files into a briefcase to relive the dream, a cup of tea in hand and clouds in view.

"Libbie?" Vivian, my chief of staff, says.

"You snuck up on me."

"It's called having your back."

"First night with Libbie in a long while," I say. "When's the last time you saw Sam in a dream?"

"My birthday. But he's always there amid the shade." She extends an arm over my desk and points to the briefcase. "You're going on recess, not to a conference. Remember your plans for a true sail, chasing the endless horizon?"

"Written in ink. Logged on my phone." I somehow got through an entire summer without much time on the water. Soon I'll be putting the boat in storage. "Those files are for the train ride, up and back. Here's the real question. When are you going to spend a few days with your grandchildren?"

"A master at changing the subject." Vivian folds her arms and raises her chin. "Melville said salt air preserves the mind for clear thinking. There'll be a test when you get back."

I MAKE my way through an Amtrak car looking for an open seat. Ahead I spot four members of the New York delegation facing each other across a table, with documents spread out amongst them.

"Madam Speaker," I say to Desi. "A leader's work is never done."

"The future beckons, Nate, and it won't take no for an answer," she says. Desi fist-bumps an elbow since my hands are occupied. "But we *have* approved a bill that addresses some of the most pressing needs of our time. Now, you and company and a few friends across the aisle just have to agree to it."

"Many of those friends see their duty to advise and consent as all consuming," I say. "No room for legislating. But your bill has a comprehensive menu, touches lots of bases.

Town hall ovations and ribbon-cutting selfies pop off the pages. There may be hope."

Desi pokes at the air with her right hand. "That's the idea," she says. "A range of programs, serving diverse needs. They're as basic as a Lazy Susan and as expansive as a second language."

Our confab is blocking traffic in the aisle. Walking backwards, I move on toward the next car to avoid stopping progress. "Three score and four years ago, a wise president pledged to help make the world safe for diversity," I say.

Desi forms a megaphone with her hands. "It begins at home."

STARTING EARLY Saturday morning, I travel from my place in Rumford, Rhode Island, to Sakonnet Harbor, where I moor my sailboat, a keel knockabout. Heading east, in the direction of the Elizabeth Islands, I sail south of Cuttyhunk on the way to Martha's Vineyard. A strong wind from the southwest allows me to make good time on a beam reach for most of the trip.

Sailing sustains me through a mix of tradition, practiced skills, and the allure of a new venture. A sailboat is a vessel to untried waters, unique in place and time. Each advance of its bow taps the unknown. It can fashion familiar sights into fabulous via an elixir of light, atmosphere, and perspective. Or it can snap a seeker to attention with a slap of spray.

I get to Edgartown in the late afternoon and check into the Jebediah Mayfield House, where I've stayed before. My boat has a cuddy cabin, but the quarters are cramped and suffocating and the accommodations minimal. While nothing tops a view of the stars stretched out in the cockpit of a boat as it rocks on water, the room at the inn has a deck with a hammock that delivers much the same experience.

Not having eaten all day, I decide to go out for food and beat the dinner rush. Pedestrian traffic is light. It's already the first weekend of October, after all. Ahead, on the other side of Water Street, a man in a Panama hat is gyrating a cane. He's looking in my direction and shouts something jumbled, ending with, "Excuse me."

I wave back and cross the street walking toward him. He has a barrel chest, but his white-tufted, spindly legs appear taxed by the weight. One hand is leaning on a storefront as the other holds the now planted cane.

"Thank you, thank you," he says as I join him on the sidewalk.

"Everything okay?" I say.

"Yes...well, no. I hate to impose, but would you be so kind as to tell me where you're dining tonight? I'm here with a group, and tonight's my turn to arrange dinner."

"Of course," I say. "No problem. The Salty Scupper. I'm going there now, actually."

"Is it on the water? They all insisted I find a restaurant with water views."

"Yes. It's on Dock Street. The front room has a panoramic sweep of the harbor. You can see the ferry too."

"Perfect. That snooty place, Poseidon Grill, it was empty," he says, as he lets go of the storefront and removes a cellphone from a pocket. "But they said they'd be full in an hour and couldn't fit us in. Rude. Please, just wait a moment if you would."

The man holds the phone out by way of explanation, ambles a few steps to an empty bench in front of an ice cream shop, sits down, and starts texting. Giving assistance without needing fifty people to agree feels good, and I'm in no hurry. He finishes the message and extends a hand. "Whittaker, Walt Whittaker," he says. "Many thanks."

"Nate Tourneur," I say, shaking his hand. "It was nothing."

"Wrong. Things that surprise hold value. Let me show you an example." Unburdened of his dining assignment, he leaves the bench with a lighter step and moves down the block to a seafood market. In the window is a water tank filled with lobsters.

"What do you see?" Walt says.

"Something that improves the taste of mayonnaise and hot dog rolls."

"Immediate pleasure has its place, but amassing a treasure of knowledge takes time. In this instance, however, time itself is the reward. Put simply, but profoundly, frozen lobsters can be brought back to life." He underscores the statement by tapping his cane against the window. "I have empirical evidence."

"If you're selling an investment opportunity, my risk-taking ends with the FDIC," I say.

"I'm a scientist, not a huckster," he says. "Twenty years ago, I observed it for the first time. Fourteen out of one hundred survived the freezing process. It involved an initial lowering of metabolism in frigid sea water, followed by an immersion in minus-forty-five degree brine. Since then, I've played around with adding various chemicals to the brine and raised the revival rate to over thirty percent."

"Still not commercially viable, although you could eat the failed test subjects. That's not something you'd do with mice."

Walt tilts his head so far back the brim of his hat forms a halo. He appears to regret having asked me for help.

"It's about science," he says. "Life-sustaining science." He centers the cane, places both hands on its grip, and leans forward, the supplicant turning assertive. "Think of all we've learned from NASA's programs—the moon landing, the space station, the launched telescopes, the rovers on Mars. Cynics would say we could have built millions of affordable housing units instead. They ignore the enhanced quality of life brought to billions from space-generated knowledge and advances."

"Close to a billion people worldwide still struggle for survival," I say. "Another billion barely subsist. We need to do both."

"More one than the other. A path to achievement is always there for anyone willing to dedicate themselves. Collective drag from the many can impede fulfillment of the best and brightest."

I feel I'm back in Washington. This conversation is not clearing my head for creative insight, or whatever it was Melville said.

"History has taught us that the so-called best and brightest need to think beyond themselves and their concentrations of capital," I say. "The many aren't demanding lobster."

"That's the problem," Walt says. "They're a dump of diminished expectations." He raises the cane to his hat brim and pivots away. "Best wishes for your evening."

"And you, yours," I say to the cane.

CHAPTER 2

At the Salty Scupper, I find the main dining area overlooking the harbor is closed until after five-thirty, but I'm welcome to sit at the bar or any of its surrounding tables. There's a guy at one end of the bar scrolling through his smartphone, with glances to a television screen playing a college football game. At the other end is a woman nursing a drink, waiting for someone or deep in thought. She is not looking at the football game. The odds for one of them trying to start a conversation with me are high, even if I sit in the absolute middle. Following Walt, I'm not in the mood, so I take a table with a pinched view of the inner harbor, facing away from the bar.

Within a couple of minutes, a waitress takes my order, and I start to browse through *The New York Times* on my phone, *The Washington Post* to follow. The woman from the bar walks by my table. I imagine she's leaving, but I'm wrong. She walks to windows facing the inner harbor, thirty feet away. She stands with hands on hips, cocks her head, and checks out the view. I return to an article in *The Times*.

"Is that the yacht club?" someone says.

I look up to see who asked the question and find the woman from the bar, still by the window, staring at me. Her legs are apart and her right arm is fully extended, a finger pointing out across the water.

"Yes," I say. "That's the yacht club."

"Why are there not more boats?" she says, as she approaches my table.

"It's October. Lots of people dry-dock their boats right after Labor Day. To everything there's a season."

"I do not believe that," she says. "May I sit down?"

Her drink—what's left of it—is still at the bar. I convince myself that she only has a couple of questions and does not want me to have to look up at her while we talk.

"Certainly," I say. I rise to pull a chair, but she beats me to it and spins around onto the seat in a move that looks rehearsed.

"I believe that to everything there is a reason. Season be damned. If you have a boat, you must have a house. And if you have a house on the Vineyard, from everything I have seen, you should use it as often as possible."

"The chamber of commerce would agree, but most people—even the residents of Edgartown—have jobs and careers that don't allow that."

"They should work remote. It is a spectacular day. Get that boat back in the water."

"Lawyers, doctors, global traders, developers, filmmakers—they all have to physically be somewhere else. At least some of the time."

"They should make the time. Make more time."

"That's the ticket," I say. "Keep on ticking."

The waitress brings my dinner. My companion declines to order anything and refuses an offer to take a portion of what I have. She does accept another drink, rum on the rocks.

"I am truly disappointed," she says. "On the one hand the beauty of this place blows me away. Rolling meadows yielding to views of whitecapped seas. Dunes and bluffs defined against the sky. But then, I want to join others in celebration. Parade down to a beach and start a bonfire. Raise sails and plane over some waves."

"You want people? Visit the museum."

"That is definitely a Sunday thing," she says.

"Or come back in August. You'll find flocks of them."

"That is what I hear. Maybe too many."

Yes, lady, even crowds, and you may not want to celebrate with all of them. I'm thinking I may have to order a drink myself but resist the urge.

"So, which are you?" she says.

"Sorry?"

"Wall Street banker? Surgeon? Film producer?"

"I'm a lawyer."

"Must be a senior partner if you are here in October."

"Actually, my position is junior in standing, but I do have some extraordinary perks. Mondays and Fridays are often half days. Dozens of staff assistants are assigned to support me on projects. My job goals and productivity objectives are loosely defined and subjectively assessed. And performance reviews are only conducted every six years."

She pushes her chair back and slaps her palms flat on the table. That gets my attention. More to the point, it gets me looking into her unblinking gaze. Two can play this game, but I blink first. I'm still facing her, however.

"That is definitely a crock, yet one incredible wish," she says through a smile. Incredible, I agree, but I should tell her it's actually true. More incredibly, her smile makes irrelevant everything else she has said.

"Speaking of seasons and time and reason, there's a concert tonight at the Old Whaling Church," I say. "Canaan's playing, one of an endless string of low-key farewell gigs. The church is a landmark, and their music made a mark, a long, long time ago."

"I know. I saw them during the first reunion tour. I was at Fenwick, in Connecticut."

"I was there, too. You must have been seven or eight. My fifteen-year-old friends and I got a college kid to drive us down from Rhode Island."

"I went with someone who was a huge fan."

"It must've been your father."

"No," she says, a smile taking the memory in another direction. "But I cannot go tonight. My friends are expecting me." She looks at a clock above the bar. "Oh, bummer. I have to meet up for a ride."

She's on her feet and away, but stops, turns around, brings her palms together over her head, lowers the joined hands to below her chin, and bows.

THE OLD Whaling Church was completed in 1843. Its clean interior lines are topped by a ceiling with the gentle curve of a vessel, held up by an unseen framework of rafters, posts, and struts. There are no pillars. This piece of architecture was raised by the same local shipwrights who built clipper ships and whalers, bringing the world to New England. A trompe l'oeil mural of a place beyond the chancel invites the faithful to walk through a wall to reach their destination. As I take it all in, the surrounding fifteen-foot windows allow this evening's twilight to grace the space.

I'm in one of the last pews, lucky to have gotten a ticket. Even in October, there are many Canaan fans on the island. David Crossley is absent for the first six numbers, which are ably rendered by Roger Mills on electric twelve-string guitar, Chris Dash on mandolin, and Gene Jung on acoustic guitar. Crossley meanders on stage before the seventh song, seemingly surfeited with sinsemilla and searching for something. He finally locates it: a tambourine.

Lifted by a standing ovation, Crossley finds footing mid his bandmates and contributes a fluid tenor to their harmonies, adding rhythm with the tambourine. They close out the show playing half a dozen hits and return for an encore, to perform "Thinking Young." Most everyone is on their feet for the final lines: "Bearing age is how you deal, thinking young's not so unreal—Steaming engine pulls the wheels, time and distance start to peel—Done with hours on the merry-go-round, younger days were more unbound—Steepled chimes due course will sound."

I feel a tap on the shoulder. It's my friend from the Salty Scupper.

"Got here late," she says. "They let me into standing room for free."

"The best concerts are always the free ones."

"It must have brought back memories of Fenwick," she says.

"My sharpest memories are never far away," I say. "Like right now."

She takes a step back, taps her forehead three times, and draws her finger in an arc toward, but not touching, me.

"Hold that thought," she says.

She explains that one of her party connected with someone on the Vineyard, a college friend none of them has seen for years. They are heading out to Katama for a nightcap.

"I *will* see you again," she says, flashing the smile. "How can I not? We keep running into each other."

I feel a little of the confusion David Crossley exhibited as he searched for the tambourine, but I lack his blitzed-out bliss.

SUNDAY MORNING, I hop a bus to Vineyard Haven to visit the Martha's Vineyard Museum. It's at the site of a former US Marine Hospital, built in 1895 and decommissioned in 1952, having treated soldiers and sailors through two world wars. Positioned on a hill, the museum has vistas of Vineyard Haven Harbor, Lagoon Pond, the bridge to Oak Bluffs, and the East Chop Lighthouse.

I'm here to view an installation on Lois Mailou Jones, an African-American artist of the Harlem Renaissance who spent summers on the island. She painted seascapes, landscapes, and other works. Those include city scenes from Boston, New York, Paris, and Washington, DC, where she taught at Howard University, as well as abstract works and mask motifs from time spent in various African nations. Many years back, Libbie and I saw a few of her paintings at the museum's old location in Edgartown, and I'm hoping those works are included in this new show.

People are already lingering in the first gallery. There's one painting I keep coming back to as others move on. It's a seascape seen from a cliff at Aquinnah. Diffused sunlight projects images of clouds onto the water, which themselves emanate glare. Fractured resolution of the projected clouds also reflects waves, the color and light conveying movement. Swirls of green lace the blue sea. A sailboat with a towed tender emerges in the distance out of the confluence of waves and glare. Its form is a silhouette amid all that light, a force defined by sharp lines of shadow, spied beyond buildings on the cliff and the vibrant green of plant life surrounding them.

In the second gallery are three pictures I recall from the past. Two feature sailing and fishing boats in Menemsha Harbor, while the third depicts vessels along the Vineyard Haven waterfront. I sit on a bench to scroll through picture files on my phone, remembering that Libbie had asked me to photograph one of them. Finding the shot, I look up to see if it's the same, but an older couple and a woman with a broad straw hat are in front of the work in question. I approach the painting and peek around the straw hat to confirm it's the one, capturing boats under sail.

"This is exactly what I was expecting," says the woman in the hat.

The cadence is slower and the tone subdued, so I don't recognize her until a face emerges from under the brim.

"You like this painting?" I say.

"So much, I would like to take it home with me," she says, stepping away. I follow.

"I should apologize for yesterday," she says. "I drank

much without food. It is a bad habit, but I have a thing about watching what I eat."

"You carried yourself well," I say. *Very well.* "I had no idea."

There are notes of a Spanish accent in her speech that I didn't pick up before. Her avoiding contractions may mean she honed English within the confines of a ballet company or concert halls, away from television.

"It asserts the glory of life," she says, looking back at the painting. "Sails billowed, lines taut, boats heeling against the wind, goals on the horizon."

"For me, it does all that and more," I say, turning for a final view. I catch her reading my eyes.

I walk around her slowly, in a complete circle.

"What are you doing?" she says.

"I want to see if there are any strings tied to you today. Friends, friends of friends, drinking buddies."

"Not yet."

"Then let's go sailing," I say. "I'm Nate Tourneur."

She beams her smile in full wattage.

"Sarita."

SHE COMES aboard wearing a laurel pullover and matching baseball cap, her dark hair in a ponytail hanging through the back of the cap. Large, wrap sunglasses shield her face. I give her a foul weather jacket since we'll be sustaining a good deal of spray from choppy seas.

Sarita knows her way around a sailboat. Hauling in a genoa jib in gusty air is a chore, but she cranks a winch to trim the sail perfectly on an upwind course. An unused spinnaker halyard comes loose and is whipping the mainsail. I'm going to steer the boat into the wind, luff the sails, and take care of it. Before I do, with the boat heeling, she secures the jib sheet, rises from the gunwale, leans against the mast, and steps onto the base of the boom. From that perch, she stretches to grab and cleat the end of the loose halyard, as we hold course.

Having passed Cape Pogue, we are heading south toward Wasque Point on close-hauled tacks. Plowing through waves, as well as the blustery conditions, make for a noisy cruise, sail edges snapping. Sitting side by side on the gunwale, though, we can talk without raising our voices. We discuss landmarks and geography for a while. She spends time trying to make out Nantucket after I point to the southeast, but it's difficult to nail more than a chimeric coastline.

"Tell me something we agree on," she says.

"We appreciate sailing," I say. "Your turn."

"I loved that painting. You did, too."

"Yes, I did." *So did Libbie.*

"Another one," she says.

"I try to be true to myself. I think you do, as well."

"Yes, I do try," she says. "But sometimes it is hard if you lack capabilities."

"I don't see you lacking capabilities."

"I should have been a biologist. Then I would have learned more about protecting and prolonging the gifts I was given."

"To benefit others," I say.

"To benefit myself, and others through my example."

I lift my voice above the chop and talk past her toward the bow.

"You don't look like you need any help. Besides, you've got plenty of time."

"What do you mean by that?"

"Go back to school. Get a biology degree. Do research."

Sarita lowers her head and speaks into the cockpit.

"To be honest," she says, "I gained more from life experience than I would have in school. But I am obliged."

Her last line hangs in the air for a few beats. She slides over to the winch to crank the genoa jib in a bit tighter, flattening some creases in the sail. She returns to the spot by my side, holding the jib sheet taut.

"How are you obliged?" I say.

"Just being dramatic," she says.

"I hadn't noticed."

With her cap pulled down and sunglasses a mask, Sarita fronts the visage of a sage, wise beyond her years.

"The demands of living," she says. "Nothing more. Besides, the conditions we endure, we often enjoy. The flip side of the same coin."

"If you say so. Right now, *I* would be much obliged if you'd take the helm, so I could raise the spinnaker. We'll have a nice run back to Cape Pogue before heading into the harbor."

WE TRAVEL by cab to Eastville Road, my favorite restaurant on the island. It is fairly empty since it's a Sunday evening in the fall, but the setting is enhanced by the time of day. Its broad southeast view of marshland, inlet water beyond, is luminous, with rays from the setting sun shimmering off the wetlands and bay. A bank of windows opens the entire dining room to the vision. Sarita dances in twirls across the breadth of this illumination before taking a seat at our table and blessing the decor. Elegantly wrought pinpoint chandeliers, reimagined whale oil lamps, miniature signal lanterns at each table, and sailing ship spars suspended from the rafters are all to her liking.

"Thank you for arranging this," she says.

"I called ahead and told them a serious critic was on her way."

She is wearing a strapless black dress and blanketing her shoulders with a silk scarf bearing images of calla lilies, their green stems showing above the rims of adobe vases. Her hair is knotted up in a twist. She raises a glass of water and gestures for me to raise mine.

"To living," she says.

"To life," I say, touching my glass to hers.

I mention that the restaurant owners operate two other places. Besides receiving high marks for their cuisine, they have reputations for supporting their staffs with decent pay and benefits, as well as promoting from within.

"I enjoy hearing that," she says. "I have friends that run companies—some of them quite large—who treat their employees like family. Privately owned businesses. Holidays are observed, and the children can join in the festivities. All birthdays are celebrated, and everyone gets cake. In the summertime, there is a play camp for the kids, and, often, amusement rides are brought in. Entertainment, too. And relatives are given preference on job openings, to maintain family ties."

"Sounds encouraging," I say. "The thing I dislike about public companies is their preference for satisfying stockholders—who do nothing—over employees. Get your staff on board the mission. Respect their contribution. Respect their needs. The profits will follow. Your friends' companies, do they provide advancement opportunities? Skills training?"

"Well, I know the workers are shown what to do," she says. "As long as they keep doing it, they have a place. They are not just numbers, discarded at the whim of management, the way public companies fire people. The worse thing they suffer is having to take a pay cut, but only when profits are down."

"I have to say, that is often the bone of contention. Are profits really down? What's *good* about public companies is the degree of financial disclosure. Labor negotiations gain from transparency."

Sarita opens her menu wide and holds it out far, like an older person who forgot their reading glasses.

"I see what I want," she says, focusing on me and basking in twilight reflected off the menu. "As for transparency, trust in those who know and count your blessings. They will continue to care if you perform assigned tasks. Our task tonight is to place orders, trust in the chef, and enjoy a carefully and beautifully prepared dining experience."

Her face dazzles with another revelatory expression that embraces the two of us, like limelight. It's enough to put to bed my desire for discourse on the rights of workers. That can wait till some other time.

"How do you do what you do with your smile?"

"It's the magic hour," she says. "The time when beauty lives to its fullest."

WE ARE back in Edgartown looking for a bottle of wine, but the package stores are all closed. There is a bar, however, at Mayfield House, where, as it happens, she and her friends are also staying, not in the original mansion, but in newer rooms built around the pool.

Sarita remains on the Mayfield House porch while I go inside to get two glasses of wine. I come out to find her at the eastern end of the porch, standing tall, an arm stretched high on the corner post. She is gazing at Lighthouse Beach and the ocean beyond, marked by moonlight on ripples. Her hair is down, a pin having been pulled from the twist. I hand her a glass and comment that she must be cold, having folded her silk scarf into a choker after we traipsed around in search of a bottle.

"This will warm me up," she says, sipping from the glass. "I wish we could sit somewhere and look at the Milky Way."

The inn's porch ceiling, a light blue, complements views of the sky during the day but blocks the stars. I invite her to follow me, and we walk a path of crushed shells to an exterior staircase at the back of the mansion. Up the stairs we go to a landing at the second floor level, and she holds my glass as I climb to unhook the fire exit door of the deck off my room.

Sarita puts the glasses down, walks to a corner of the deck, and tosses her hair to take in the sky. She spreads her arms, hands on the rail, bathing in the beam of a full moon. Wind blows through nearby hickory trees, and she folds her arms. I put my jacket across her shoulders, and we sit down by a table.

"What do you like about me?" she says.

"Your lack of patience," I say. "Your youthful exuberance."

"I am not a youth."

"Neither am I, but there are times when my spirit flags, and I feel a lot older than I am. I detect a fire in you that keeps doubts at bay. It seems you've found a way to stay connected to your young self, the you that debuted as an adult."

She sipped her wine as I spoke, sips some more, and sits back, my jacket sleeves draping over her.

"When you commit to something, you commit," she says.

"Going for a sail and having dinner aren't major commitments."

"They show a willingness to engage when much remains unknown," she says. "You have a feeling for adventure."

"That depends on what, and with whom."

She sits up, pulls the chair closer to the table, and extends her hands.

"Show me your palms," she says.

"I don't believe in fortune tellers."

"But you believe in me," she says. "I am going to recite lines from a poem. Look at me as I say the words."

She holds each of my hands and presses her thumbs against the inside of my wrists. Our knees touch, and she peers into my eyes.

"Rising one day to an imposing encounter," she says, speaking slowly. "Bearing the weight from an imposing encounter, fighting the spell of an imposing encounter."

Ten seconds pass. She continues to hold my hands.

"Do you have anything to say?" she says.

"Crisp and cryptic, but I don't know what it means," I say. "I'd have to read the whole poem. I hope I passed the audition."

She lets go of my hands but stays focused on my eyes.

"With flying colors," she says. Then she looks for and finds her glass and takes a swig, glancing back at me. "I wish you could see what I saw."

I laugh and sample the wine.

"My view wasn't bad, either."

The wind is picking up. A weathervane atop a gable is pivoting.

"Starting to feel the cold," she says, rubbing her forearms. "We should go inside."

I retrieve the key fob from my jacket, and she carries the glasses, much wine remaining in both. With the screen door at my back, I pop open the entrance and let her go in first. I enter, shut the main door, and hear the screen banging back and forth in a gust. Just as I'm about to reopen the door to lock the screen, it slams shut and clicks its latch. None too soon.

THE BELLS of the Old Whaling Church are ringing, and I count seven, but likely missed one or two in waking up. My arm brushes against Sarita, and I feel a chill. Probably because we had the air conditioning on all night. I unbundle and spread the blanket over her gently, admiring the shine of dark hair reaching down her back.

Gaps in tresses around her face reveal an open mouth. It's possible she's awake. I kiss her cheek. It feels cold. Her lips don't move. She's not breathing.

CHAPTER 3

Sarita's eyes are closed. I spread the hair back from her face and gently rock her by the shoulders. No reaction. My ear is on her chest. I hear nothing. Pressing her wrists, I wait for a pulse. Maybe I'm pressing too hard.

Under the black dress, lying across a chair, I spot her spaghetti-strapped clutch. There's a mirror under the lid. I place it by her mouth, then beneath her nose. No fog on the glass.

I call 911 and get routed to voicemail. Finding the EMS address, I jump into slacks and a shirt and run out onto the deck, door left open, the screen slamming behind me. I take three stairs at a time down the fire exit.

Two men are standing by an umbrella table in the yard, each drinking from a demitasse, saucer in hand. They are startled as I pass. Looking back, I say, "EMS," meaning to explain what was up.

I sprint out to Water Street and keep sprinting. Every hundred yards I slow down for a set of deep breaths before sprinting again. The sidewalks are mostly empty, and the intersections free of cars, except at Main Street, where I slap the hood of a moving SUV and dash past.

My feet hurt. I'm thinking it's because I haven't run this

hard in a long while. Feeling more pain, I sense my toes and realize I'm barefoot.

I turn right onto High Street. By the next block, I can see the fire station up ahead. Getting there, I find the station doors open and all the garage bays empty. Inside, I learn about a major fire at the retail center on the Edgartown-Vineyard Haven Road, involving a supermarket and some other stores. All the fire department and EMS personnel are there.

I sit on a park bench, facing the sidewalk, my eyes filled with tears. *She's dead. Admit it, she's already dead.* Teardrops fall into splotches of blood. Uneven bricks along the way have cracked the soles of my feet. Stretching my arms over the back of the bench, I look skyward then close my eyes to screen visions of Sarita—at the Salty Scupper, the concert, the museum, in the boat, at Eastville Road, on the deck at Mayfield House, last night. Eyelids open, I go through the sequence again and recall different moments, replaying things she said, very much alive. But looking down at the blood, I know that her death is not a dream.

Obtaining cash from an ATM, I walk to a nearby shoe store, which opens at 9:00 a.m. Parked on another bench, after a while I hear the bells of the Old Whaling Church toll nine. Getting the attention of a salesperson, I purchase a pair of slip-ons and socks, paying for the transaction out on the sidewalk.

I head back to Mayfield House taking my time, superficially because of the aching in my feet. When I reach the inn, I stop at the driveway to let a black SUV with tinted windows exit. The shotgun seat window is down, and its occupant may be one of the men I saw earlier with the demitasses. I nod, but he does not return the gesture. He looks away as the window rises. Wrong guy, or perhaps he doesn't recognize me with shoes.

I ascend the staircase to the deck and take a moment to imagine her standing by the rail, staring at the stars. I think of her seated at the table, wrapped in the embrace of my jacket, and later, rubbing her arms to lessen the chill.

Steeling myself to reenter the room, I open the screen door and blink to adjust for darkness out of sunshine. I blink again. Sarita is not on the bed. Oh, happy day. I check the bathroom. She's not in there either. The dress is gone. She's taken all of her things, scarf, shoes, and purse. I go to the hallway, search around the corner, see no one, then head for the first floor reception area. Galloping down steps never hurt so good.

There is one woman at the counter and another seated at a desk. I address the woman at the counter.

"I planned to meet up this morning with a good friend, Sarita Montoya," I say. *Whose full name I only learned last night.* "She's also staying here. Would you please ring her for me?" I smile and spell out the name, as asked.

"We don't have a guest registered under that name," she says.

"She's staying with friends," I say. "A group of young women."

"How young?"

"Sorry," I say. "I should've been more specific. Early to mid thirties."

She turns to the woman at the desk. "Any groups here this weekend?" she says. The other looks up, shaking her head. "Not that I know of."

It crosses my mind that she may have used another name, for whatever reason. I can hardly suggest that about my "good friend," and, in any case, it won't help right now.

"Look, I met her here in the lobby yesterday to go out for a sail," I say. "And again, in the evening, before we went to dinner. She had on a black, strapless dress."

"I wasn't here yesterday," says the woman at the counter.

"I wasn't here either," says the other one.

"What does she look like?" says the counter woman.

Grasping the edge of the counter with both hands, I exhale a quandary, looking left then right. I'm about to say she has long dark hair but remember that it was under a cap while sailing and afterwards was gathered in a twist, until later. I don't know how her hair is right now. I could add that even in a loose dress the arch of her back speaks volumes. That she moves as one elongated muscle, like a puma. That, when she holds a pose, it's as sleek as marble. That she can fix a gaze, adjust her eyes away, then return the look, as if to say, "I'm ready, are you?"

But all I say is, "She has dark hair."

Both women laugh.

"That's not much to go on," says the woman at the desk. "Could you give us some identifying details?"

The investigative language deflates me.

"You're right," I say. "Not much of a description, and anyway, it's not important. Should you happen to see a dark-haired woman under forty, alone, please ask if she's Sarita Montoya. Tell her Nate Tourneur wants to say goodbye. I'll be here for another hour."

"Aren't you the weather guy on Channel Four, the one that covers the hurricanes?" the counter woman says. "Standing out in the storm, with all the waves crashing around you."

"No, that's not him," the other says, smiling at me. "You do the sideline interviews during the Patriots games."

Leave it to the vox populi to knock one off one's pedestal. At this moment, being brought down to earth is decidedly a good thing.

"Sorry to disappoint, but no, neither one. And I regret bothering you. Thanks for listening."

Regret, indeed. I return to my room. What's happening? The situation has gone from tragic to a miasma of intrigue. It's great she's alive, but I have questions. Like, how did she lower her blood pressure and slow her heartbeat? Is it a Zen thing? And, just as pressing, why did she leave? I search the room for anything that might provide a clue, either to Sarita or her disappearance. Nothing. She left without a trace.

I shave and shower and pack. Getting ready to depart, I want to cushion my shoes with tissue, to reduce impact on the bruised feet, but the tissue box is empty. I look in the cabinet under the sink in the bathroom and locate more tissue. Removing the box, behind it I find a communications device with a strap.

Close examination reveals it to be a microphone, not a recorder. So, someone else was listening to, and likely capturing, our conversation.

I start running hypotheticals. Blackmail? Media provocateur? Gotcha journalist? Cuban spy? Did she take pictures during the night?

We didn't discuss politics, and I revealed no government secrets. But, of course, audio could be edited to produce embarrassing statements, especially if made in the company of a spy. Being caught in bed with an agent—or even a lobbyist—would raise the ante considerably. If that's the angle, though, she could have detached the mini microphone from the strap and kept it by her pillow, instead of dumping it in the bathroom. What *was* the angle? I have much to think about on the next leg of what started as an invigorating, getaway sail.

The women in reception have nothing to report concerning my darkhaired friend but have succeeded at their own investigation.

"You're a senator from Rhode Island," says the one at the desk, pronouncing it "Row Die-len," as so many do.

"I knew I'd seen you on TV," says the other.

"That's right," I say. "Thanks again for listening to me. I very much appreciate it."

Out the corner of my eye, I see an older woman struggling to open a glass door at the side entrance. She has one hand on the door grip and the other on a large piece of luggage. It looks like an upright, hockey goalie's duffel bag on wheels and is as tall as she is. I rush over, open the door, drop my backpack outside, and pull her black bag into the lobby.

"Thank you," she says. "This thing is such a nuisance, but I don't like to fold my dresses."

"I'm sure you have one for every occasion," I say. "Have a pleasant stay."

Picking up my backpack, I notice two demitasses on the umbrella table in the yard where I had seen the men earlier. And again, at least one of them, in the exiting SUV.

I snap my head around to squint through the glass door and focus on the large black bag moving through the lobby.

It had to be them.

CHAPTER 4

ailing in a steady wind on a port tack, I'm about two miles south of Nomans Land, a small, uninhabited island off the west coast of Martha's Vineyard. Headed for Block Island, I may not arrive at its harbor until after sundown but already have a hotel reservation.

Tugging in the sheet to trim the mainsail, I think of Sarita alighting on the boom to retrieve the errant halyard and how she handled the challenging genoa jib with skill. Today I'm using a simple working jib on a traveler, a device for getting by alone.

I steer the boat into the wind and let the mainsail luff. The jib is flapping as well. I move forward to the cuddy cabin, open its double doors, hook them back, then slide the mounted entryway hatch toward the bow. Yesterday, when I stored the spinnaker after our sail, I smelled a dank odor in the cabin. This is a day to air it out.

Once again at the helm, I lay off the wind, the sails fill, and the boat is back on course. Fingers dry from days of sun and saltwater and handling lines flash me back to this morning. Sarita's cheek felt parched when I kissed her, and I detected a hairline scar in the skin along the jaw, as if something had once slit her complexion.

I realize I made a mistake in squeezing her wrists to find a pulse, the way she squeezed mine as she recited the poem. It would have been better to check a carotid artery in her neck. I would have been certain sooner.

How did a young, physically active, and, to all appearances, healthy person suddenly die? For at this point, I believe she died. Was she drugged? Given a slow-acting poison to kill her in my bed? If so, to what end? "Senator Wakes Up With a Dead Woman" is a riveting headline, but where's the body?

That said, her corpse might yet show up somewhere else. Whereupon, I'm thinking, a planted discovery of pictures of us together—for assumed blackmail purposes—could be used as evidence that I had her killed. Or killed her myself. Talk about a headline. Even my search efforts with the inn staff would be seen as an attempt to fake an alibi.

But such a plan, as imagined, is convoluted, distended, and open to logistical questions. Where might her body be left that would be in proximity to the places we had visited together? How would it be done without attracting notice, and surviving a timeline scrutiny of witnesses who had seen the two of us? No, if Sarita's death was intentional, scandal would most surely have derived from her murdered self remaining under the covers with me.

The fact that her body was removed, however, does not negate the possibility of a crime. The presence of the microphone, her mysterious disappearance, and the demonstrated facility with which her body was likely removed from the inn via luggage—I left the deck door to the room open when I ran to get EMS and did not return for over an hour—all suggest criminal activity.

To what end, though? I revealed nothing that compromised national security and opined on no issues that might be construed as politically damaging. Moreover, as a widowed man with no current partner, being in bed with a woman is not cause for scandal. That is, unless the woman's ties to others call to account my integrity, ethics or sworn loyalties.

Sarita may or may not have had dodgy connections, but if dishonor, disgrace, or embarrassment were the objective, her body would not have left my bed. Associates removed her because her presence jeopardized not me but someone or something else. Her death by natural causes upended plans, forcing them to act. What were their plans? What *are* their plans?

As I dwell on the possibilities, a mechanical whir gets my attention. Out of the western horizon I spot a helicopter coming east. I'm guessing it's headed for Nantucket. If you want to beat the traffic and a sluggish ferry, flying is the way to go.

The helicopter veers southeast as it gets closer. That's strange since there's nothing out there, unless you're planning to land on a ship. It passes me to port on its southerly turn, and I figure that's got to be it, giving it one more glance before looking forward to adjust the mainsail. A southwest wind has become brisk but not enough to stir up chop. I'm making good time, the bow rising and falling in rhythmic advance. I fix the mainsheet in a cam cleat, the limp end remaining in my hand.

Upwind of the departed chopper, my mind is free to reconnect with the imbroglio of Sarita and the mystery men.

I recap our conversations, searching for telltale phrases, barbed replies, and pointed questions. The poem that she recited last night on the deck looms largest because it emerged as a late step in our bonding. I keep coming back to the phrase "imposing encounter," occasionally voicing it as a mantra in the hope of eliciting an answer.

Deep in thought, punctuated by those chants, I'm surprised by a downwind eruption of chopping from a helicopter. I turn my head to find that it's only two hundred yards astern and no more than fifty feet above the water. It flies lower as it nears, and I see legs hanging out from its fuselage. The chopper approaches on the starboard side of the boat. The air it churns, bouncing off the water, blows dents in the curve of the mainsail. The extended legs grow a torso and arms. The arms are holding an automatic rifle aimed at me.

I dive under the starboard gunwale and flatten myself on the sole, as shots ring out and wooden coaming splinters around the cockpit. The chopper passes beyond the mainsail, and more shots are fired. Storage boxes under the port gunwale are obliterated.

I grab a bungee cord from netting and slide underneath the transom, at the stern. As sound of the helicopter moves on, its view is blocked by the perforated but still functioning sails. I tie the cord onto the tiller, to steer while under the transom, and try to camouflage myself with a seat cushion.

The helicopter reappears to the south, making a wide turn back toward the boat. It flies past, and out of my line of sight. I guide the tiller with the cord to stay on course with sails filled—the mainsheet still clamped in the cam cleat—and the boat making headway. I need momentum.

The volume of the rotor's chopping pops is louder. A shadow of the helicopter falls across the port side, into the cockpit, and onto the mainsail. The boat's cabin doors, hooked open, are rattling under the pressure of chopper turbulence. The entryway hatch is shaking. I see the outer edge blur of rotor blades, hovering lower than before. Churned air adds force to the sails, increasing speed and allowing me to point up toward the wind, nudging closer to the helicopter.

As I pull the tiller to the starboard side, hard to leeward, turning the boat directly into the chopper's path and thrusting the mast into the rotor blades, a smoke trail zips through the cockpit to the cabin. A rocket explodes, launching the boat's mast even higher within the death zone of the blades. Caught in the chopper's rotational maelstrom, the mast's wire stays gyrate like a weed cutter, scratching the deck, severing the tiller cord, and slicing through the seat cushion that is my camouflage. The aluminum mast groans and screeches in the throes of its duel with the blades. Neither wins.

The ebbing loss of lift causes the helicopter to bob and weave for a distance, then crash, cockpit first, into the ocean. I see the fuselage flip over onto the rotor and blades, with all their entanglements—spars, sails, lines, stays—and sink.

The bow of my boat is totally blown off, the cabin with my bag and phone is under water, and the rest of the hull is slipping fast. I stand on the raised stern, glance at the name, *Resolution*, turn, and dive away from the wreckage.

I'm treading water against an anxious urge to swim off, waiting to see whether anyone pops up from the sunken helicopter. If a survivor rises with a gun, I'll be better off staying close, as opposed to thirty yards away, able to sub-merge deep and come up on them from behind. I count off the time for about three minutes. Nothing.

Behind me I hear an upward burst and spin around. The wooden cabin hatch, loosed out of its track, shoots length-wise from the sea, falls over, and floats by my side.

Relaxing in this good fortune, I take a moment to search the 360-degree horizon for a vessel but am not surprised to find none. It's a Monday afternoon in October. Kids are in school, adults are working, and fishing folk are further out.

Aided by the hatch, I'll make good time swimming the distance to Nomans Land.

HAVING FOUND a damaged pram—a chunk of its stern is missing, where an engine mount would have been—I'm scavenging the shoreline of Nomans for driftwood boards, one to use as a paddle and others to prop up as a wooden sail. Sitting forward should lift the damaged stern and keep seawater out.

An island of about 600 acres, Nomans was formerly used by the navy for bombing practice. The US Fish and Wildlife Service now manages the locale as a wildlife refuge. For that reason, and the risk of unexploded bombs, public use of the island is prohibited.

I spot what appears to be a sign at the top of a bluff. Climb-ing there, I see that it reads, WARNING – RESTRICTED AREA - US GOV'T PROPERTY. I'm able to dislodge the single post on which the small sign is mounted. Descending,

I discover boards settled among the backs of boulders just above the shoreline.

Placing the boards upright between the pram's flat bow and the first crosspiece, I jam them secure using other driftwood and remnants of plastic floats and foam buoys, capping this base with my hatch.

I set off in the rowboat from a spit of sand and tide-worn stones that is Nomans' closest point to Martha's Vineyard. The upright boards catch a southwest breeze blowing toward the island, and the sign atop the post works as an adequate paddle. I make a mental note to send a contribution to the Fish and Wildlife Service.

THE SUN is setting over the Elizabeth Islands as I reach the Vineyard, north of Squibnocket Beach. I walk along the shore and then the path to the Aquinnah shops to get cash from an ATM, buy some snacks, and take a bus to Oak Bluffs.

On Circuit Avenue I purchase fresh clothes and a jacket. The events of the last twelve hours have me on edge. I look away as I hand the cashier my credit card, hoping she doesn't pick up on the combination of my name and face. While I usually don't mind being recognized, I do find that it hardly ever happens when I'm not in a suit and tie, even in Rhode Island. It's more likely, as recently shown, that I'll be seen as a weatherman or a sportscaster. She gives me back the credit card without comment, and I go to change in one of the dressing rooms.

Across the plaza, I visit a convenience store to get a notepad and a pen. I also buy a faded teal cap with a stitched image of a sailboat. Upon exiting, I stop to tuck the pad and pen into a jacket pocket and pull the cap visor down. Standing halfway between Norma Sue's and the post office, I hear an outcry, then a screaming crowd, but there's hardly anyone in the area besides me. A mob appears around the corner from Kennebec Avenue, rushing through the plaza. An older man slows and steps into the alcove created by my presence.

"Is it the running of the bulls?" I say.

"I wish," he says. "No. A skunk founds its way into the middle of the line at Screen Door Desserts."

The crowd thins, and I head to Natalie's, by the harbor, for a lobster roll to go. It reminds me of the man with the cane, Walt Whittaker, and his resurrected lobsters. I finish it on a bus to Vineyard Haven, where I board the day's last ferry to Woods Hole. From there I'll travel via a Peter Pan bus to Providence, with connections to New York, and ultimately, Washington.

TRAVELING SOUTH on Interstate 95, my bus passes an exit for Quonset, Rhode Island, reminding me of an interview I gave to *Narragansett Nautical*. I told them that when things get overloaded and tense, my safety valve getaway is a sail to Martha's Vineyard. A local magazine with, apparently, wide circulation. Who knew?

After crossing into Connecticut, a sign appears, SCENIC VIEW AHEAD. I look out the window toward the coast, searching for the view, but you can't see much at night, even if it's Mystic.

I'm jotting down notes about the last three days. Earlier I concluded that Sarita's body was removed because her dying by my side had jeopardized someone or something else. Evidently, the danger is so serious that I had to be taken out, as well, with my attempted murder most definitely premeditated. Why?

Forget what I might have said to Sarita, because none of it was material, outside of my interest in her. Rather, what did she say to me that imperiled others? They tried to kill me since they knew I wouldn't stop digging.

I review quotes from her that I've written down: "prolonging gifts I was given...I am obliged...just the demands of living...we often enjoy what we must do... trust in people who know and be grateful...they will care if you do what is asked."

Taken out of context, some of the words carry import, but are hardly ominous, and nothing specific. I keep returning to the refrain from the poem, "imposing encounter." With that, the context was everything. Holding my hands, thumbs on my wrists, a focused stare, asking for my comment afterwards. The setup was of a piece with the antic, stop-and-go nature of her seduction.

That was the point. Even in the heat of infatuation, certain behavior could give pause, tapping the brakes against getting it on. The slam poetry, presented as something of a lie detector test, was one such moment in the screwball movie of our time together. Put on notice, I was alerted to be alert, subjectively regarding a pending tryst, and objectively regarding knowledge of the truth behind "imposing encounter."

Since I have no idea what it means, I passed the audition. Some people, however, were concerned I *might* have known. Sarita's death tipped their hand.

I have work to do, finding out what it is I should have known. Getting some sleep will help, but it's difficult sleeping with lights on above nearby passengers. More affecting, still, is the extinguished light of a beautiful smile.

CHAPTER 5

Tuesday morning in Manhattan I purchase a burner phone and text Mike Levien, my chief speechwriter and senior legislative director. I ask him to call ASAP, then sign off with "ICU," our office's alert signal. Five minutes later he calls, as I'm getting to the Twelfth Avenue terminus for interstate express buses.

Without discussing Sarita, I explain that my boat was sunk under suspicious circumstances, omitting the violent context. There's no need to cause undue worries. To keep things under wraps, I instruct him not to say anything to Vivian or other staff members but ask that he contact just one person. Lastly, I want him to pick me up in Baltimore.

"Email Mick Golden at DHS and see if he knows anything about the possible code words, 'imposing encounter,'" I say.

"Imposing encounter. What's involved?"

"I don't know. It appears to be important to the people who sunk my boat."

"Anything else?"

"Don't tell Mick about the boat. Just say I had a run-in with some devious characters on Martha's Vineyard, who made veiled references to an imposing encounter."

"I guess if there's something to it, he'd be able to steer us in the right direction."

"Exactly."

"But that's not much in the way of details."

I hear concern in his voice about contacting an under-secretary at DHS over a relatively minor incident, based on the little I've shared.

"Don't worry about Mick," I say. "He and I go back a long time. That's why I only want you to reach out to him, so I can control this until we know more."

"Got it."

"I should be at the BWI train station in a little over three hours," I say. "Mention to Vivian that you're not feeling well, and you're going to work from home for the rest of the day."

I'm taking a bus to avoid running into someone on Amtrak who knows me, including conductors and staff. Likewise, asking Mike Levien to meet me at Baltimore's BWI station. It's important that the attackers, or, rather, their associates, think that I died and disappeared at sea. You can't trip up people who aren't going about their business undeterred.

BWI STATION is relatively crowded for noontime. I'm on a bench reading a hard copy of *The Washington Post*. There are no stories about a helicopter gone missing off the coast of Martha's Vineyard. That would require a slow news day under the best of circumstances. From a reporting perspective, the circumstances for dredging up the story, let alone corroborating it, are far less than best.

As I turn a page and refold the paper, from under the visor of my hat I notice five people standing in front to me, a woman and four men. The woman steps forward.

"You need to come with us," she says, understated but direct.

"I haven't finished *The Post*," I say.

She moves closer and takes the paper.

"Paying by cash or debit card?" I say.

A man to her right opens his jacket to flash a holstered pistol. A man to her left grabs my arm, pulls me from the bench, and says, "This way."

"Of course," I say. "I've grown attached to my arm."

We move as a group through the lobby.

"Just keep quiet," says the man who flashed the gun.

"Do that, and I'll be dropped from the chat room."

My dance partner leans in and says, "Stop the noise," as he squeezes my arm.

"You call this noise?" I say. "I was born in a hurricane."

"Enough," he says.

"Someone's coming to pick me up," I say. "They'll be disappointed if I'm not here."

"That's their loss," the woman says.

"You should expand your worldview," I say. "Losses can cut both ways."

"I like my chances," she says.

"Do you see yourself as a den mother or the leader of the pack?" I say.

"At the moment, you're all I see," she says.

There's a Rio Grande lilt in the voice.

"I should've freshened up."

Outside, we are walking by a multilevel parking garage, the man still holding my arm. People are exiting an elevator inside the garage. I pull loose and run toward the exterior rear of the elevator shaft. Passing it, I circle round to the front, as two pursuers go by, and rush into the elevator, pressing the button for the highest floor. There are no other passengers. The focused leader of the pack appears through the crack of the closing doors. She slams the outside as the elevator rises.

Exiting into the open-air top level, I look around and see three girls, a man, and a woman at the back of a minivan, loading suitcases. I walk in their direction to the front of the car. The young women are nodding their heads and saying, "Kamsahamnida," as the man arranges the luggage and moves to shut the rear door. They're expressing thanks in Korean. As a politician, I've learned to say thank you in a dozen languages.

I get into the driver's seat, start the engine, put the car in gear, and drive off toward the exit ramp. The woman catches up with me, screaming, but I don't know enough Korean to understand. She tosses a cup of coffee across the windshield as I enter the tight confines of the exit ramp. In the rear view mirror, I spot the leader of the pack emerging from a staircase and dashing in pursuit. I also see the cause of the car owner's rage. There's a toddler in a harness strapped to the back seat.

Speeding down the spiral ramp, the child crying all the way, I reach the ground level, but the two main exit gates are backed up with other cars. There's a third exit for taxis that's currently free of traffic. I'll have to drive over a raised sidewalk and bust through a weighted barrier to reach it, then smash the gate. As I'm scoping this out, two of my new friends from the pack spot me and charge from across the street, one of them holding a pistol tight to his thigh. The toddler is too young to be press-ganged. I get out of the vehicle and salute goodbye to the kid.

"Thanks for the lift," I say.

Sprinting to the tracks, I reach the end of a platform and leap onto the track bed. Behind me, a northbound Amtrak train is slowly leaving the station. Ahead, on a track to the left, a southbound train is approaching fast. A horn blows at my back, but I continue to run in front of the locomotive, eyes focused on the arriving train. I glance behind and see the pack giving chase, the leader out front.

The engineer in the southbound train is glaring at me, probably cursing, and punches the horn as I bolt across his path, like a glob of beach plum jelly squirting from a perfect PB&J sandwich. The trains seal the gap, creating a barrier between me and the pack. I've escaped two trains running but have to pull up short at a ten-foot chain link fence topped with barbed wire.

Climb the fence, or bang a left to the platform on the southbound side, momentarily protected from my pursuers by the arriving train? Before I can decide, a head slams the small of my back, sliding past the right hip, as arms embrace my torso, and a shoulder shoves me to the ground. A textbook tackle.

There's a knee on my spine. My face is introduced to the trackside refuse of bottle caps, cigarette butts, and candy wrappers, and some wind has been knocked out of me. By the time I have breath to speak, my wrists are secured behind me with a zip tie, bound faster than a calf at a rodeo.

"Are you from Texas?" I say.

"San Antonio," says the leader of the pack.

She helps me to my feet, brushes off some dirt and dead grass, and places the hat on my head, pulling down the visor.

"You're lucky to be alive, jumping through those trains," I say.

"I was following your lead."

Inside their vehicle, I'm seated in the middle row, side by side with the Texan, as we set out on a highway. She reaches into a storage console and turns to me holding a knife. Its purpose is a known unknown, but I tense up from the downside potential.

"Aren't you going to play the Deguello first?" I say.

"What?"

"The Deguello. Music will give me a chance to think happier thoughts. Maybe I'll fly out of here."

"What are you talking about?"

"You said you were from San Antonio. Remember the Alamo?"

"Oh," she says. "El Deguello."

"My accent must be off."

"No, no, no," she says, pointing the knife at the floor and shaking her head. "I'm sorry." She nudges the bound hands from behind my back and cuts the zip tie. "You're okay now, Senator."

"Tell that to my back," I say.

"There are protocols," she says.

"Apparently, those are shared on a need-to-know basis," I say. "I guess I don't have your vote."

"You'll understand after the briefing. That's all I can say."

Neither she nor any of her associates says much else before we pull into the basement garage of the FBI headquarters in Washington, DC.

CHAPTER 6

'm sitting alone at a conference table in a windowless room waiting for Mick Golden to arrive. Mick is Under Secretary for the DHS Office of Intelligence and Analysis. He was two years ahead of me at Annapolis, but we played on the hockey team together. He was the goalie. I was a defenseman. Our paths crossed again at the Office of Naval Intelligence.

My hunch that "imposing encounter" is a loaded term, possibly a codename, was more than confirmed by the reception committee that escorted me to FBI headquarters. That the agents wore no insignia and didn't otherwise identify themselves shows my detainment was meant to be without notice, my efforts to the contrary aside. I know the helicopter attack on me was intended to be deadly. Now I know that the greater plot from which the attack sprung is potentially lethal to an elevated degree. Moreover, it's beyond the planning stages.

Mick Golden enters the briefing room, followed by others. Seeing me, seated at the middle of the table, he rushes over as I rise to greet him.

"Nate, how are you doing?" Mick says. "Sorry about earlier today."

"I'm fine," I say, noticing that the leader of the pack, changed from pursuit clothes, is now among the others in the room. "No worries. I realize the bureau has protocols."

"Yes, but it was me that set it in motion," Mick says. "My office at DHS is about analysis. Our boots on the ground are only in play if you cross the border without papers, or try to bring a weapon onto a plane. This was an unusual situation. I needed assistance."

"You got plenty," I say, eyeing the leader of the pack, who's taken a seat by an end of the table. "I may have put them through their paces, but I met my match."

"Don't worry about Mr. and Mrs. Yang," says a voice behind me. "We settled their grievance."

It's Badge Newcomb Prescott, FBI Assistant Director for Counterintelligence, who comes into the room through another door. He represents the fourth generation of his family in federal government service and, prior to his present post, spent years at both CIA and the State Department, having started his career as an agent with the FBI.

"Feel fortunate you didn't damage their car," he says. "We have budgetary limits for such things, as you should know. What were you thinking, Senator?"

"I was more concerned about the child in the backseat," I say.

"You kidnapped a child?" says Badge. "You didn't say anything about that, Pilar," looking over at the leader of the pack, whom I now know as Pilar.

"From what I saw, the Senator was acting as a babysitter," she says.

The deadpan delivery may be an expression of regret for my rough treatment, or perhaps it's just her sense of humor.

"Effectively, that's true," I say, nodding at Pilar, whose face is impassive but her eyes are focused. "As for what I was thinking, Badge, it appears this meeting's been called to give credence to apprehensions I've developed over the last twenty-four hours. Something to do with an imposing encounter."

"Quite," says Badge.

I sit down. Mick sits to my right. Badge takes a seat on the opposite side of the table, joined by Josh Kuhn, Director, CIA Middle East Mission Center. Others find seats on the periphery.

"First, Senator, would you be so kind as to brief us on the who, what, where, and how you developed these apprehensions?" Badge says.

"The few things I have to share, Badge, will resonate more once I have dots to connect them to," I say.

Badge taps a pen on a folder he brought, silently staring at me.

"The situation has a basis related to Iran," Mick says. "But the level of its direct agency, if any, is open to question."

"Although still on the table," Badge says. "Let's hear from the CIA. Josh?"

"Surveillance of nonstate actors in the Middle East is signaling that a long anticipated event has finally reached the execution stage," Josh says. "We're expecting an act of reprisal for the killing of General Kharrazi."

General Javad Kharrazi was personally targeted under a US action more than two years ago. Our government justified the assassination as a response to violent attacks against US forces in the Persian Gulf region, attributing them to insurgent militias in Iraq, Lebanon, and Yemen supported by General Kharrazi and Iran.

"You'll recall that Iran's immediate response was to launch missiles against our bases in Iraq, with a number of troops suffering injuries," Josh says. "After Iran forces subsequently shot down an airliner by mistake, half-filled with Iranians, street protests in Tehran seemed to bring the matter to a close. Yet, principals within Middle East militias that Kharrazi assisted continue to vow revenge."

"That's what this is about?" I say.

"Motivationally, yes," Josh says. "We're not certain of all the links, but it's possible Iran has turned a blind eye to terrorists tapping components of its international network to exact retribution. Kharrazi remains an heroic figure there. A blow struck with him in mind—regardless of who's responsible—would be welcomed by most Iranians."

"You're picking up reads, leads, and internet chatter from parties with ties to Iran, but you don't know if it's directed by Iran," I say.

"We can't be sure that official Iran even knows about it."

"Face some facts, Senator," Badge says. "The morass of the class of people in the mix congeals like an upside-down cake, like Denver pudding. Double agents are given amnesty and protection by third parties that were once their enemies. Who's on first?"

"But you're certain something serious will happen in the near term," I say.

"More than that," Badge says. "While Iran is probably not behind it, intelligence is clear and unambiguous that a severe action against the United States is imminent. Imposing Encounter is the tag."

"Weeks?"

"Days," Badge says. "So, what do you have to say. Given you more than a few dots to connect to."

He's correct that it's my turn to talk, but that last, cheeky comment doesn't sit well.

"Why wasn't the intelligence committee briefed on this?" I say. "It's a national security threat."

"The Gang of Eight was briefed," Mick says. "It wouldn't be prudent to tell the entire senate committee. The White House wants to limit access since the president may yet decide on a course of covert action."

That's why they believe Iran isn't the instigator. Although we don't have diplomatic relations with Iran, an entreaty ultimatum must have been delivered through Switzerland and Pakistan, our contact intermediaries. An implied US response—as a covert action—would have been so catastrophic that a good faith answer from the Iranians was more or less assured.

"How can he act, covertly or otherwise, if we don't know who's driving the attack?" I say.

"As chinks in the armor are exposed, closer to the endgame, active response will be made, wherever the openings lead us," Josh says.

I let a moment pass.

"I met and spent time with a woman on Martha's Vineyard," I say. "After a number of conversations, over two days, she recited a poem, asking me to pay strict attention. The poem was a test, to see if I knew anything about Imposing Encounter. I did not."

"Why did you ask Mike Levien to contact me if the words meant nothing to you?" Mick says.

"By then, I knew ulterior motives were at play. I came to that realization after the woman died, and her associates tried to kill me." I look over at Pilar. "That's why I was less than cooperative today." She holds my look without expression.

All in the room sit fixed. No one makes a sound, until Badge coughs.

"Do you...?" he says, coughing again, then speaking in a strained voice. "Do you have a picture of this woman?"

"My cellphone went down with my boat," I say. "But anyway, I didn't take a picture of her."

"A pity...I mean, we could've run the photo to ID her," Badge says.

"How did they try to kill you?" Josh says.

"I was sailing south of the Vineyard, on my way to Block Island, when I was attacked by a helicopter. A man in the side bay shot at me with a rifle. On the second pass, the chopper was low, so I sailed into it, to stick the rotor with the mast. At the same time, they fired a rocket. The bow exploded, and all the rigging got tangled in the blades. The chopper crashed, sank, and no one came up."

"How did you avoid getting hit with debris?" Mick says.

"I caught a break." Looking across at Badge, I say, "By the way, I can give you coordinates. You could raise the chopper for details, if your budget allows."

"Seeing us fishing for something at the site would tell others you're alive," Badge says. "Right now, for your country's sake, it's better you remain dead, metaphorically."

"I prefer fictionally."

"The result is the same," he says.

"Fictions come to an end, metaphors linger," I say.

I'm processing what I've just learned. Their surety that an attack is pending is hiding behind soft-pedaled references to Iran and a broad allusion to links. While it's easy to imagine the general's allies among insurgent militias—commanders, foot soldiers, couriers, scouts, scroungers, spies, forgers—using a mutually created network to hatch a plan of vengeance, they're giving me no details. I'm being briefed on a limited basis, particulars withheld.

"About the woman, what happened?" Badge says.

"She died in Edgartown," I say. "Some men absconded with her body from my room, while I was out getting EMS. I later learned that she had lied about certain things."

"How did she die?" Mick says.

"I don't know the cause of her death," I say. "She was dead when I woke up."

"You know you entertain risk consorting with questionable individuals, Senator," Badge says.

"I doubt she had security clearance, if that's what you mean," I say. "But it's not like I visited a brothel in Louisiana or participated in the sex trafficking of 17-year-olds in Florida. And if she sensed I knew something about operation Imposing Encounter, what's the worst that would've happened? The attack would have been called off or postponed."

Seeing frowns form on the faces of Badge and Josh, I think of something else.

"Your source would've been compromised," I say. "You have an embedded agent."

"Along those lines, yes," Josh says.

"And you're relieved things happened in reverse. Their agent's death exposed deceit. They killed me, so to speak, to hide my discovery. Now you want me to stay dead."

"Yes," says Mick. "For a week or so. You're a man who knows too much."

"If they sense we're on to the plot, our agent, close to contacts in the game, will be a suspect," Badge says. "Exposed as guilty, elimination would follow."

There's a source, an agent close to people on the other side, at a place they know, providing details of a plot to attack the United States, but they are sharing none of that with me. I will have to find out more on my own.

"A week is a long time," I say. "I need to be productive."

"Certainly," Mick says. "Copies of pending legislation, research materials, whatever you want. We'll bring it to the safe house."

"I want to go to Puerto Rico, to follow up on information the woman gave me. It could add to what we know. You could assist me in not blowing the cover of my fake demise."

"Not good," Josh says. "Too much exposure, too much risk, for little gain."

"That's a lot to ask, Nate," Mick says. "Everyone in the room is dealing with this situation, and some of us have more besides."

"I'm not asking you as a friend. This is a request from a senator. If you won't help, I'll go to Florida by bus and catch a plane from there. Believe me, no one at the ticket counter will pick up who I am."

"Anything she told you was fabricated," Josh says. "She was coached."

"I don't agree. She shared things that rang true. She disclosed leads I want to follow. I survived an attack and want to make something of the time I've been given."

"If he's willing to travel by our rules, under protective identity, I don't have a problem," Badge says. "Need to send a minder, of course."

"Senator Tourneur was the best penalty-killing defenseman I ever played with," Mick says. "Composed, communicating. Knowing where everyone was on the ice. Blocking shots with his body. Catching the opposition overplaying their advantage with breakaway steals. He even scored a couple of shorthanded goals." Mick turns to look directly at me. "But now is not the time for you to take risks. You're not ONI anymore."

"I took risks because I was playing in front of a top-rated goalie," I say. "I'm not ONI, but in my present job I swore an oath to defend the Constitution against all enemies, foreign and domestic. And I'm sure the minder Badge mentioned won't be a slouch."

Mick sucks on an imaginary lozenge and settles back in his seat.

"Josh, anything else?" Mick says.

"I defer to Badge," Josh says. "He did survive Damocles' sword."

"So far, so good," Badge says. "But, Senator, now having more than one life to lose for your country, give some thought to remaining dead for the long term. Set you up in a program with a very nice home in a place of your choosing. Might possibly satisfy the other side—a senator for a general. Could save some lives."

"Maybe I'll consider it if you fully share with me what we're dealing with."

I look at Badge, Josh, Mick, and all their associates around the table. No one raises a hand to speak or utters a word.

CHAPTER 7

t was after midnight, during my time with Sarita, that she told me her last name, Montoya, and described her early life in Cayey, Puerto Rico. Dancing at festivals made her a local celebrity and opened up performance opportunities elsewhere. I have enough information to seek out facts that will fill in what she sketched and trace a path from those beginnings to her expanded horizons. From there, I hope to find answers to what brought her into the company of terrorists.

Before leaving for Puerto Rico, I speak with my aide, Mike Levien, to brief him on the basics of what happened at BWI Station. He himself was picked up by FBI agents on the way to his car an hour after emailing Mick Golden.

Per Badge's directive, Mike will work from home for the next week and discuss none of these matters with anyone. The story is he's nursing an illness. He'll be under watch around the clock and will limit outside trips to his neighborhood.

Then I call Vivian Perske, my chief of staff. Without going into details about my sunken boat or mentioning operation Imposing Encounter, I explain that I was drawn into a severe security situation, and that this threat will cause me to be out of reach for a number of days. She should not let on to staff members that anything what-soever is wrong.

"Stay home," I say. "It's recess."

"That's the plan," Vivian says. "I just came in to catch up on my backlog."

"For you, the future's a backlog. Go home. That's a direct order."

"You're not in the navy anymore, Senator," she says. "Although someday you'll have to tell me how you found yourself on the front lines."

"Public service," I say. "One more thing. I'm totally fine, seriously, but certain not-so-nice people think I've been killed."

There's silence for a few beats.

"So that's the meaning of severe security situation."

"Right, sort of," I say. "Like falling into a reverie. You never see it coming."

"I'll make a note of that."

"It's not as bad as it sounds, but as of now, the word is I must remain dead."

"Are you in a hospital?"

"No, I'm fit as a fiddle at sundown. The idea is that the other side should think they succeeded in an objective."

"How can I help?"

"What would you have done if you hadn't heard from me by tomorrow morning? No call, no text, nothing."

"I would've texted 'Silence is golden. Keep sailing.'"

"And if I didn't respond?"

"After an hour or so, I'd contact the inn on Block Island," she says. "See if you checked in."

"They say no. What next?"

"Confirm that you checked out of the inn on Martha's Vineyard. Did you?"

"Yes. Then?"

"I'd reach out to Hannah Curley in the Providence office, touching base, no big deal."

"She has nothing to report," I say.

"Somewhere, stress levels are rising."

"I know. I'm sorry. What next?"

"I call the state police in Rhode Island to convey my concerns and submit my findings," she says. "I explain the circumstances and ask them to keep a lid on it until they've had a chance to complete an initial investigation. After they do, I imagine they'll suggest we contact the coast guard."

"That's it. The only thing I ask is that you wait one more day. Don't call or text me until Thursday."

"Should anyone check, they'll see it doesn't match our routine, even on vacations."

"It won't lead to that sort of inquiry," I say. "I plan to be back among the living next week. Are you ready for something else?"

Another moment of silence.

"If this call goes any further south," she says, "I'll have to put on sunglasses."

"There's a chance you'll be visited by a person saying they're an old friend of mine," I say. "By your home or on Capitol Hill."

"In that case, Lieutenant, I'd feel cozier in the office."

"I understand. Again, I'm sorry. Hopefully, they never come. But no one could handle this as well as you."

"It's clear to see how you get votes," she says.

It's not easy to ask someone close to join the front line when they never signed up for it. Yet it would be far worse to not ask and expect her to deal with whatever happens, leaving her totally in the dark. That would be a breaking of trust.

"This person will absolutely guarantee they're a classmate, either from St. Margaret, Moses Brown, Annapolis, or Columbia Law. Told I'm away, they'll want to know when I'm returning, since they're only in DC for a few days. They'll press hard."

"The point being, they'll weigh the emotions behind my rote responses of back next week, all is well," she says. "They'll look for the suppressed pain of someone expecting the worst but clinging to hope regardless. I've been there."

CHAPTER 8

Tuesday evening, I fly to Puerto Rico with a minder, Special Agent Pilar Cruz. Badge Prescott probably assigned her, my dauntless captor, as a dig on me. I'm concerned, though, that she may be upset to leave the inner circle working on operation Imposing Encounter. Instead, she claims to agree on the value of investigating Sarita to determine her ties to the plotters. Or maybe she's just saying that to ease any tension that might arise from having to guard me.

As for the big picture of an imminent threat, she won't tell me anything I don't already know. She does admit to factors that remain unknown, such as where it may occur and the type of action. The essentials haven't changed: a severe attack on the US by a network of terrorists.

I've been given identification documents for an alias, Jamie Boone, which Pilar says was selected by computer under a bureau algorithm. I was not asked for suggestions.

It's after eleven by the time we arrive in Old San Juan and check into our hotel, El Claustro, a seventeenth century building that was once a cloister for nuns. The night is warm, and a breeze carries scents of flowers mixed with salt air. Since we'll be leaving for the town of Cayey early in the morning, I want to take a walk around the ancient city, established in 1521 on an island linked to Puerto Rico by bridges. Pilar offers to join me.

We find a vendor selling green coconuts by the Plazuela de las Monjas, in front of the cathedral. He chops off the tops with a machete and uses an ice pick to poke holes for straws. Bearing refreshment, we head out to explore, and not just the city.

"You do know she was acting," Pilar says, talking about Sarita. "I mean, maybe she let her guard down and divulged information, but she was playing a role."

"She may have taken on a role," I say. "But her own life experience informed the performance."

"That's a distinction without a difference," she says. "As far as we're concerned."

"I don't think so. It adds a dimension that points to her motivations. Her own life choices."

"Give me an example."

"I expect to confirm things she told me about her upbringing. One set of fixed dots. Then I hope to learn about her initial escape. Another set of dots. Those two sets, mega dots, define a line. Motivations that produced the line are likely consistent with the behavior I saw. More importantly, those motivations are a clue to her involvement with terrorists."

"We're looking for hard connections to the people involved," she says. "Her choice to fall in with them is not the puzzle we're trying to solve."

"Not the principal puzzle, but if we find out what attracted her, it'll help draw a line to parties that met the need."

"Profiles have their place," she says. "It could be, though, that she simply liked to act, and was good at it."

"There are venues for that."

"She might have been good but not good enough," she says. "Or she had issues—debts, addictions. They paid her when others wouldn't, or gave her drugs. Plain and simple."

"The nuances that characterize people are rarely simple," I say.

"Okay. I take back the simple. But I know people who react to life's losses by cutting out risk. They narrow the scope of what they do to things they can do well. Things that are appreciated by others. Like locking yourself in a role."

"As you said, profiles have their place."

We come upon a white home marked as the Casa Blanca, now a museum about Juan Ponce de Leon's descendants, who lived there during the sixteenth and seventeenth centuries.

"It was being built while Ponce de Leon was still alive," she says. "But he died before it was finished. He's buried in the cathedral."

"So, he never found the fountain of youth, yet he lives on through his reputation. Another way to survive. His legacy."

"There's no historical proof he searched for the fountain," she says. "He was after gold and seizing people to work on plantations. The usual."

"Gold buys you a cushy lifestyle, and forced labor dumps physical pain on others," I say. "That's one way to stay young."

"He put down a few uprisings, where he slaughtered and enslaved lots of Tainos. Then he was killed by Native people in Florida who didn't want to be colonized. He's definitely remembered. I wouldn't call it a legacy."

Walking toward battlements overlooking the bay, we enter the Plazuela de la Rogativa. The little plaza holds a group statue commemorating a procession during an attack by British forces in 1797. Thousands of civilians, women and men, participated in a prayer march, carrying torches, singing hymns, and ringing bells. The Brits thought the commotion signaled an arrival of fresh troops and sailed away.

Lighting around the plaza casts shadows, magnifying and multiplying the four figures in the sculpture. Standing by a stone sentry box, we take in the scene amid an expansive view of modern San Juan, lit up across the bay.

"Democracy in action," I say.

"It was a religious event," she says.

"Religious overtones, but civilian people were the power."

"Many believed the end result was an act of divine intervention," she says.

"Here on earth God's work must truly be our own. A president said that."

"Marching and singing can only accomplish so much," she says. "Work that brings results means flying to Puerto Rico for clues about a dead woman's ties to violent extremists. Using that info to confront killers head-on."

"The British captured Trinidad easily two months before," I say. "Here, they landed troops and launched bombardments, but both sides were well matched. Puerto Rican civilians on the march gave them a glimpse of the future. They cut their losses and withdrew."

"Naval history is not naval intelligence," she says. "Reacting in real time means scanning forward not back. Staying focused on a six-day window and not flinching from what needs to be done."

"Like tackling a senator who misread signals," I say. "I get it. But past stands against oppression ripple into the present. We ignore them at our peril."

"I ignore nothing, Senator."

DRIVING OUT of downtown Cayey, we're looking for a white church with green louvered doors within a gothic arch entrance. Sarita said it was the first place she sang solo in public. Her residential barrio, where she grew up, should be a few miles further south, on a winding road heading up into the mountains.

Finding the church, we take a left turn, over a bridge spanning a river, and begin an ascent to higher ground. The roadway landmark for the barrio is a convenience bodega across from a bus stop. We reach it in about ten minutes and pull over, off the pavement, into a puddle, evidence of a severe thunderstorm that rained through the night. There's a large, lid top refrigerator outside the front of the store under an awning, which is still dripping. Two men sit nearby playing dominoes.

Inside, I find a young attendant who speaks English and ask whether he knows of Sarita Montoya, a singer-dancer-actress who grew up in the barrio. I tell him we're journalists doing a magazine story. Behind me, I hear Pilar speaking to someone in Spanish. My guy says no, so I ask him to question an older man seated by the counter, who's reading a newspaper. Translating his answer, the attendant tells me the older man knows the name but hasn't seen her for a long time. Pilar taps me on the shoulder.

"Look at what I found," she says, holding up a framed photograph. "There are three others in the back room, but this is the best. My friend here says she's the one in the green dress." Pilar gestures to the gray-haired gentleman at her elbow. "Is it her?"

The photo is an eight-by-ten color glossy, taken on the set of what appears to be a TV soap opera. The woman in the green dress stands back from a man and a woman in the foreground, staring intently at one another.

"It could be her," I say. "The big hair throws me off. Maybe it's a period piece."

"Or a retro series," she says. "Like *The Aughts Show*. The good news is that her brother lives nearby."

Back in the car, we take a left off the main road and proceed up a steep incline that continues for half a mile. The brother's place is at the very end of a country road. The incline extends to the front porch of a farmhouse, on which sits a white-haired, sleeping man.

We wake him with pounding steps up the front stairs and a loud greeting of "Buenos dias." Introductions reveal his name is Teodoro. I make a few mumbling statements invoking Sarita, entwined around the Spanish words for singer, dancer, actress, and, finally, sister, abruptly amended to daughter. Pilar steps in to calm the bewildered man and convert an incoherent interrogation into an engaging conversation. I realize that without her presence I would've had to drive him down to the bodega and ask the attendant to translate an interview.

From what I can glean, Pilar appears to be making progress, but Teodoro speaks very slowly. On the other side of the road, I notice a stream and a hill beyond. I recall Sarita saying that she and her siblings and cousins would swim after picking crops. Interrupting Pilar, I explain that I'm going across the way to check out something.

I take off shoes and socks, roll up my pants, and wade into the water, walking downstream. Just as she had described it, I arrive at a natural pool formed by eons of erosion over stone and the protection of surrounding boulders. A narrow outlet feeds a miniature waterfall.

Reaching the far bank by stepping on stones and scrambling over boulders, I return upstream to a trail and proceed to climb the hill. The slope is steep but barren, which makes for an uncomplicated ascent, though I search in vain for signs of the tobacco leaves Sarita said she picked. From the summit I see Las Tetas, a pair of volcanic peaks that mark the Sierra de Cayey range.

"Mountain breezes supplied a bit of chill to the Spanish soldiers stationed here, back in the day," Pilar says, joining me as I take in the view. "Although that probably didn't help much in July and August."

"Let me tell you, any breeze at all would help get you through a hot day in uniform," I say. "Like baseball making bases bigger four years ago, cutting the distance between first and second by inches. Stolen bases surged. From small things big things come."

"What are you looking for?" she says.

"Tobacco," I say. "She used to pick tobacco. Filler leaves, the ones curled inside of cigars. The source of their aroma."

"No, thank you," she says. "Although out here, up high in the open air, it might not be so bad."

"Some people like the scent of cured leaves, without lighting them up," I say. "In any case, the US in the early twentieth century imposed specialization in cash crops for export. Tobacco, sugar cane, coffee, rice. The idea was a more efficient use of limited cropland."

"Let me guess," she says. "Not a lot of the export cash trickled down to the people."

"Worse," I say. "The island's small size ultimately meant that it couldn't grow enough of any crop to remain competitive internationally, pricewise."

"And that, indirectly, led to the tax incentive for pharmaceuticals to move their operations here."

"That was a big part of it, producing jobs," I say. "Did you get any information from Teodoro?"

"I did," she says. "We have to go to Arecibo to follow up on what he told me."

We descend the hill, cross the stream, and get in the car to drive back to the highway. I'm at the wheel since Pilar needs to search the internet on her smartphone. As for me, I'm still limited to the burner phone I got in New York.

"So, she was a member of his family," she says. "She may have been a half-sister. His father married a second time. I can't be sure."

"Sure of what?"

"I'm trying to verify some of what he said." Pilar's focused on her phone and typing an inquiry.

It's possible, of course, that the old guy's father married again late in life and had a daughter. In generations past, farmers, whether New Englanders or Carribeños, often worked their wives to an early grave or suffered their death in childbirth. Islands were no paradise for a woman.

"Senator Nathanael O. Tourneur," she says, continuing to type. "What does the O stand for, if you don't mind my asking?"

"Open," I say.

"Open?" she says. "What does that mean?"

"To be completed."

"Like a donut hole?"

"More like the missing link."

"You're forty-one, correct?" she says.

"Are you wicked smart or just Wiki?" I say.

"You *are* a public figure."

"Target would be the better word, lately. Why are you asking?"

"What?"

"My age."

"I wasn't asking," she says. "I was confirming it. All the running yesterday at BWI. Climbing the hill today. You're much more fit than the average senator."

"The average senator qualifies for social security," I say.

"What are you qualifying for?" she says, in a tone that's less than prying but more than curious.

"Why do you ask?

"Having a job that often lasts for life, and never worrying about their next meal, many senators let themselves go. Not you."

"I think thin."

"What's your purpose?"

"Doing my job. Which includes asking questions. What have you been looking up?"

"Does PDL mean anything to you?" she says.

My eyes are on the road, but side vision is sufficient to see she's staring at me.

"PDL," I say. "What is that, another terrorist operation?"

"I saw something—Teodoro showed me something—that suggests Sarita was employed by PDL."

"Is that a bad thing?"

"It makes her a person of interest."

"Person of interest?" I say. "She's dead."

"Being part of an attempt to kill you made her a person of interest, if she wasn't fake," she says. "Now we know Sarita was real."

"I knew that already."

"You say the woman you knew died," she says. "She survives as a person of interest through a connection to PDL."

"Which is what?"

"More than what we know," she says. "We're on a fact-finding mission."

"So I can expect to learn a few things," I say.

"Me, as well."

I glance at Pilar, but she turns away.

"I have to think," she says.

That is all. She refuses to expound on PDL for the rest of the trip to Arecibo, on the north coast of the island. Her thumbs, though, stay busy. I have no idea whether she's typing search inquiries, participating in chats, or submitting reports, but her manner is intense.

The one time she interacts is to translate a weather alert, broadcast over the radio. It's been raining hard since we got on the highway. Per the report, more than eighteen inches of rain are expected to fall within the 24-hour period that began at midnight last night.

CHAPTER 9

We are parked in front of the headquarters and a production plant of PDL Biopharma in Arecibo. It's about eleven o'clock, and we're experiencing a respite from the rain. Pilar informs me that she's arranged a virtual meeting for tomorrow afternoon with Badge Prescott and Josh Kuhn. They've agreed to brief me as to why PDL is on their radar.

In the meantime, we will continue to investigate Sarita's ties to PDL. Per what she learned from Teodoro, Pilar says her duties included, but were not necessarily limited to, promotional appearances and public relations work, capitalizing on her celebrity status. Pilar's plan is to start with someone in the marketing department and try to meet Sarita's contact in the company, posing as a journalist under a cover she's used before. Depending on the results, we would then approach employees and interview them as to her recent activities, if any, on behalf of PDL.

The headquarters receptionist has us wait fifteen minutes for a young man in a suit to appear. Pilar hands him a business card and explains we're doing a story on Sarita Montoya and her work for PDL. He studies the card for too long before raising his eyes to Pilar.

"Is this just for a magazine?" he says.

"Yes," Pilar says, pointing to the card in his hand. "An online magazine."

"She hasn't made any appearances for the company recently," he says. "Of course, we value her long association."

"That's wonderful," she says. "Could we sit down and talk about her long association."

"No, not now," he says. "The marketing director would be the one. But he's not here. I will give him your request. He'll revert back."

Having achieved little with management, we're on to the rank and file. Food carts surround the parking lot, and a side lawn is covered with picnic tables and chairs, all of which are wet. Across the street is a retail center that has a few restaurants. As noontime approaches, some people begin lining up at the carts, while others go across the street.

We start with employees in the food cart lines. By the third cart, Pilar has questioned a dozen employees of PDL but found no one who has anything to say about Sarita.

Along the way, I notice a man carrying boxes to various carts from a pickup truck. At one point, between trips, he stops to listen to Pilar. He's tall and is wearing a white, ten-gallon hat. As we head toward a fourth cart, speaking in English about our lack of success, he approaches us, a broad smile bursting from below a moustache.

"My friends," he says. "You're making a mistake."

"In what way?" I say.

"You keep asking about Sarita Montoya," he says. "People around here—at least the older ones who remember her best—know her simply as Sarita."

"Thank you," Pilar says. "It sounds like you might be able to help us. Would you be willing to answer some questions?"

"What's it about?"

"We're journalists doing a story on her," Pilar says.

"Sarita? What kind of story?"

"As a celebrity...," Pilar says, glancing at me for a sound bite.

"About singers and actors who use their fame to promote, or do commercials for, goods and services," I say. "Like reverse mortgages, crypto currencies, time share properties, health care products. That sort of thing."

The man erupts with a laugh that knocks his head back. He lifts a hand to keep his cowboy hat from falling off.

"Things to avoid, except for the health care," he says.

He introduces himself as Abdul Khan and says he would enjoy talking to us but not out in the wind. He directs us to a restaurant across the street and promises to join us there after completing deliveries to food carts he owns.

The restaurant serves Japanese cuisine, and we're greeted by the sushi chef, a Mexican American who tells us he trained in New York City. He discloses that Mr. Khan, the restaurant's owner, already texted an order for us, comprised of an assortment of luncheon dishes. Although the furnishings are typical, the place is decorated with a number of striking photographs, some taken in Manhattan.

When Abdul Khan joins us, removing his hat, he explains that the photos are by a NYC artist, Katsushige Mizoguchi, whose works are in dozens of museums and university collections across the US. I comment on one in particular, an image of the Empire State Building reflected in a street puddle under the half-light of dawn. It has an aura of mystery captured by an artist alert to the ineffable.

"My favorite is over there," Mr. Khan says, pointing to a photo of two identical clocks, side by side, perched on a pair of scales. The clock on the right, indicating twelve-fifteen, weighs more than the one set at twelve-oh-five. "He was a master of visual puns and irony. I felt, as foreigners in New York—he was Japanese, I'm Bangladeshi—we were both sensitive to the tendencies of Americans. Time management is high on the list."

"You have a place in New York, too?" I say.

"Not anymore," Mr. Khan says. "I moved here many years ago. One vacation in Puerto Rico, and I said this is it." He raises both hands high and laughs, almost as loudly as earlier. "America without snow."

"What can you tell us about Sarita and PDL?" Pilar says.

"Whenever the company sponsors something, she shows up. Parades, festivals, games, award dinners, fundraisers, community celebrations. She is very popular."

"Why?" says Pilar.

"She used to be on TV, of course, in telenovelas," Mr. Khan says. "That was before my time here. You must know about that. And there's her music. She recorded some albums. I still have a couple of her cassettes. You lend them out, but they don't all come back." He smiled, shrugged, and extended upturned hands. "Her music is that good."

"Does she represent PDL in any business matters?" I say. "Product advertising? Consumer relations? Zoning approvals?"

"On business matters, I was about to say no, but in the past, going back some time, they did have a small problem. And there were complaints."

"What sort of complaints?" I say.

"PDL operates an organ donation service, for people who want their organs to be given away after they die. For this, PDL's under a contract with the government. There was a big need after Hurricane Maria and then the pandemic. They handled it."

"Did PDL do it themselves?" Pilar says.

"If they didn't, they put up with a pile of water buffalo crap for nothing," Mr. Khan says. "Some family members thought they'd get ashes back from the remains, after body parts were donated. But the bodies themselves were usually given to medical schools and research institutions."

"Were there lawsuits?" I say.

"Yes," Mr. Khan says, slapping a palm on the table, then breaking into a sardonic grin. "Their loved ones had their wishes totally fulfilled, but the relatives are screaming bloody murder."

Pilar's thumbs are moving like pistons as she types onto her phone. I can't tell if she's searching or taking notes.

"How did Sarita help?" Pilar says, without looking up.

"She was at every community meeting, every press conference, every hearing, every inquest. She would embrace the families, console them. I only went to a few—they were entertaining—but I heard from others about her constant presence."

"Was she acting officially?" I say.

"Not obviously," he says. "Sarita went among the bereaved as one of them, sharing in their sorrow."

"Performing as a grief counsellor," Pilar says.

"Exactly. Like a volunteer."

"But she was there on behalf of PDL," I say.

"Of course," he says. "Look at it from their side. The fine print of the authorization documents spelled out all the possibilities, as long as you know the meaning of cadaver. There was no way they would lose in court. But in the court of the people, her help was huge."

I think of Sarita and her comments on doing the things you're asked to do.

"Are you sure PDL was the actual company handling the organ donations?" Pilar says, still typing. "Could it have been an affiliate, a related company?"

"It's possible," he says. "I was just a bystander. I have my organs. All of them. You may be right. The alphabet's a soup of possibilities." He snaps his fingers to get Pilar to look up and points at her phone. "Check it out." He turns to me with a twinkle in his eyes. "Crazy ladies."

"Been there, present company excluded," I say, with Pilar too deep in her search to take it in.

Abdul Khan kicks an extra chair away from the table and leans back, hands gripping the arms of his seat.

"There are other things," he says. "She's the face of a spa PDL operates, near Utuado, in the mountains. I've catered some affairs up there. Organization dinners. Holiday celebrations. Private parties."

"Is it a staff facility?" I say. "A benefit for employees?"

"Why would they do that?" he says, laughing. "No, it draws wealthy people from California and New York. Even Europe. A well-known yoga group splits its annual meetings between the spa and a place in Hawaii. It's on the grounds of a parador that used to be a coffee estate."

"What's it called?" I say.

"La Fuente," he says. "And I'm sorry, it's not operated by PDL. Now I remember, the entire place is run under a foundation started by David Rashidani, the CEO of PDL."

Pilar halts her thumbs and puts the smartphone down. Right elbow on the table, she rests her forehead in the palm of her hand. A train of thought appears to have gone around a bend and reentered her brain through another tunnel.

"I was given the chance to cater social affairs after getting to know Sarita at my spice store," he says. "In downtown Arecibo. She shops there often, coming in with an escort of bearers."

"Like an empress," Pilar says, palm still fixed to her forehead.

"Others have described her that way," he says. "As for use of the spa by PDL employees, again I need to correct myself. A few times a year, daylong fiestas at La Fuente *are* organized for workers and their families, hosted by Sarita. I've supplied some of those, as well. My contacts at the company have confessed that it's in their interest to display appreciation."

Pilar has engaged her phone again, but her manner is desultory, as if she's weighing the effects of a downside revelation.

"Why is that?" I say to Mr. Khan.

"After pharmaceuticals lost the federal tax incentive, many moved on to cheaper labor markets," he says. "Brazil, China, India. By staying, PDL was able to fill open positions with trained and experienced workers laid off from departing competitors, and at bargain salaries."

"So, a handful of days at a luxurious, but occasionally vacant, spa keeps the corporate family singing the same song with no sour notes," I say.

"You sound like a TV person," he says. "One of those guys that answers their own questions."

"At least I don't laugh at my own jokes," I say with a straight face.

He raises a hand, and we high five.

"One must always deal with sour notes, my friend," Mr. Khan says. "But there's no need to make an alarm if the chorus is singing praises. These people have been through the Great Recession, Hurricane Maria, and the pandemic. They're happy to serve. Don't push."

"Not without tossing them occasional crumbs like the spa," I say.

"Crumbs?" he says. "Hours in the presence of an empress is an affair to remember."

I feel heat in my face that I believe is self-generated but might actually be coming from Pilar's eyes, whose glower I acknowledge with a look.

"Another point," he says, a smile inflating his cheeks. "I find it fascinating that, in the west, disasters are treated as being great. The Great Depression, the Great Recession. That thing that happened after the pandemic—the Great Resignation. Why is that?"

"You forgot the Great Hunger," I say.

"I cannot forget a thing I do not know," he says. "But it fits my idea."

"Which is what?" Pilar says.

"To honor suffering and pain is a weakness of government by the people. No, you should call great those who lead and achieve, who create and rule, so others can live. Cyrus, Darius, Xerxes, even Alexander."

"Only men?" she says.

"Not true. I was just speaking before about an empress. And Elizabeth, the English woman—the first one—and Catherine of Russia were truly great."

Pilar picks up her smartphone and stands, facing Abdul Khan.

"What if the suffering and pain of the people are caused by those who rule?" she says, tapping the table with an index finger. "Government by the people, for the people is the answer. The best answer."

"Such force," he says. "You remind me of Sarita when you speak that way."

"I'm not a puta," she says, leaving the table and heading outside.

"And I'm not a dog," he says laughing, as he selects some shumai dumplings for his plate. "She even looks like Sarita. By the way, which of you is writing this story?"

Stunned by Pilar's unexpected name-calling, I hadn't caught a resemblance. But yes, standing with head high, there was a fleeting similarity as she uncorked her exit line. I want to find out what's happening with her, but I don't want to give up learning more.

"She's strong," I say. "If that's what you mean about her look. I'm the writer, and the piece's for an online business site. Nothing personal. Don't worry. But about your argument on greatness, consider the Great Awakening, a religious movement that encouraged ideas of equality and individual rights and influenced our revolution. It was about empowerment, not suffering and pain."

"What kind of power?"

"The kind that gets people demanding answers to where the bodies of their loved ones have gone," I say.

"Okay, I hear you," he says. "There were answers, and some received compensation, but I must tell you one thing. A mystery was never solved."

"A mystery about what?"

"There were rumors that PDL used bodies for experiments at a research center in the mountains, not far from where the spa is. There was evidence, but investigators could not pin down an answer. Is that empowerment?"

"What sort of evidence?"

"Look it up," he says. "You're a journalist."

I'm more than that, in an elective sense, but investigative senators may find, like journalists, that certain roadblocks to a story remain impenetrable. Forces, and yes, powers, beyond our control conspire to obfuscate and insulate.

"When did you last see Sarita?" I say.

"A good question," he says. "Time here is fluid. Not like in New York. The markers are torrents and tides, rain and rivers, storms and streams. Were the mountain roads passable when I last visited the spa? Was she carrying an umbrella when she last came to my store? That's how I remember."

"If it takes that long to describe a memory, it must be quite a while ago."

"At least six months," he says. "Perhaps more. PDL has operations in Mexico, outside of Mérida. In recent years, Rashidani, the CEO, has spent more time there than here."

I ask about Sarita, and Khan responds by seamlessly alluding to the schedule of PDL's CEO.

"Are their itineraries that close?" I say.

Abdul Khan laughs and leans back.

"You mean, are they a couple?" he says. "He supposedly had a wife in New York. I never saw her here. On the other hand, I've often seen Rashidani and Sarita together, at events downtown or at the spa. But that's usually related to PDL. So, who knows?"

He's backtracking.

"That's all?" I say. "Nothing else? She's an attractive woman."

"Some people say she's his mistress," he says. "Of course, there's envy in those comments. You can imagine."

"Certainly."

"Except he's old now. That much I can tell you."

Expressing gratitude to Abdul Khan, including thanks for the meal for which he refused payment, I leave the restaurant and find that it's raining again. Pilar is sitting in our car with the engine on. Her smartphone's charging as she uses it.

"Did he add anything?" she says, not looking at me.

"Not really," I say. "Power to the people is not among his cherished beliefs."

I'm curious why Pilar's manner has turned blunt. I also wonder why the simple fact of Sarita's connection to PDL makes her a person of interest to the FBI, beyond the business on Martha's Vineyard. Reflexively, I imagine it signals PDL's material involvement in operation Imposing Encounter. Yet it could just as possibly be about the rumored experiments on human bodies Abdul Khan mentioned. Or both. I'll hold that last info close until tomorrow's conference call, on the off chance it's something I know, and Badge, Josh, and Pilar don't.

She has made reservations for us at La Fuente, the parador and spa affiliated with PDL. She gives me directions to a highway south, heading out of Arecibo toward Puerto Rico's largest and highest mountain range, the Cordillera Central.

"Did you have a lot to drink when you were with her?" she says, after we get on the highway.

"You're referring to my puta, correct?" I say.

"I'm sorry, Senator," she says.

"No problem," I say. "It was a little harsh on her."

"I apologize to you. I won't apologize to her."

"It was not a situation where I needed to be drunk, if that's what you're getting at."

"Let's let it go," she says. "It was just a question."

"Questions are the roots of understanding."

"Don't you mean the route to understanding."

"Both," I say. "The source and the way."

"Your personal business with her is outside my concern, Senator," she says. "I'll leave it at that."

"You can't leave out the personal, Agent Cruz," I say. "It's an essential part of the work we've chosen."

"How's that?"

"Advancing and defending the blessings of liberty."

Hoping she'll dwell on it, I shut up, find music on the radio, tune out the squeegee chant of the wipers, and wait for her to give me a course correction. I notice her playing with GPS coordinates on the phone. The coastal plain continues for five miles before the road begins to rise. She tells me to take the next exit.

We proceed uphill along a twisting road for ten minutes. Pilar is focused out her side window, which she keeps wiping to clear the fog.

"See that dirt road ahead on the right?" she says, pushing a finger against the windshield. "Make the turn and park where you can."

I follow her instructions, bring the car to a stop, and shut off the engine. To the west I see a creek flowing down from the slopes in front of us.

"I'm going to follow the water upstream," she says, taking a large flashlight out of a paper bag on the floor. "Up there, not too far, is an entrance to an underground river."

"I assume this has something to do with PDL," I say.

"Yes," she says, putting on a cap and a vest and sealing the phone in a pocket.

"Are you doing this because of what you learned today?" I say. "Something you didn't know about PDL before the trip?"

"I can tell you their radar blip grew larger. And another hunch I've been nursing's taken shape. Besides, I'm here. Why not?"

"A blip, a hunch, and a why not," I say. "That's how I got involved. Let's go."

"It's best you wait for me here, Senator."

"I'd rather not lose two women in one week," I say. "And I see there's another flashlight in the bag."

"It was two for one," she says, getting out of the car.

"Touché, or should I say touchy." She pays me no mind, as she shuts the door and heads up the hill.

After about fifty yards on an overgrown path, parallel to the creek, we come to an opening in the hillside. Water flows out of the vertical face as if from a tap. The edges of the entrance are masked in vegetation, but enough light penetrates to expose the interior limestone framing of a tunnel.

"This is a branch of one of the largest underground rivers in the world," she says. "The Rio Camuy. It's carved over two hundred caves inside the mountains. Many have petroglyphs created by the Tainos."

"Some of them came up here to escape the Spanish," I say. "Correct?"

"It worked for a while," she says, aiming her flashlight through the entrance.

I turn on mine. "After you," I say.

CHAPTER 10

We are able to walk along a bank of the underground river. Occasionally the limestone floor is slick, and for support we use our free hands to grab ledges from grooves etched into the walls. With two flashlights, the way ahead is clear.

Twenty minutes in, we hear the sound of rushing and falling water, even though the creek beside us is flowing with hardly a gurgle. The water noise increases as we approach a broader opening with a higher ceiling. The creek we've been tracking emerges from within the space and runs downstream toward us over a natural bridge. Greater volumes of this underground water break to the left and right into sinkholes, causing all the echoed splashing and rumbling. We stop before crossing the bridge.

"How close are we to your objective?" I say.

"I want to double the distance we've covered so far," she says. "The objective itself is a guestimate."

"It's okay with me."

We step into the water and wade over the bridge, careful with our footing to avoid slipping left or right. Nearing the flow source, we see a dry expanse of limestone floor beyond it, covered with fractured slabs, scattered boulders, and a deposited mix of rocks, gravel, and sediment. Entering this dry space, we decide to slow our advance, making sure that one of us gets over or around an obstacle before the other attempts passage. That way, we use both flashlights to guide one hiker at a time.

This obstacle course of boulders and broken rock continues for an extended stretch before the air cools and our path begins to rise, punctuated by stalactites poised overhead. Their moist presence and dripping participation in creating stalagmites on the ground remind us that branches of the Rio Camuy run above, as well as below. We are exploring a labyrinth of caves and chambers in the foothills of much higher peaks, through which headwaters spring or accumulate, converge, and flow downstream.

Ten yards ahead of me, having traversed an interval without stalagmites or boulders, Pilar stops and aims her light upward, capturing the contours of an arch. An expansive space looms on the other side.

"This may be it," she says.

"What exactly?" I say.

"That's for us to find out," she says.

We pass under the arch to discover wings extending from a center space, like transepts at the crossing of a cathedral. Directly above the center is a dome. The wing to our right ends at a chasmic pit, the bottom of which cannot be found by the flashlights. Pilar tosses a rock, and I count off four before we hear it dunk. Ripples from the void pitch tremolos that bounce faintly off the dome.

The wing on the left has a mezzanine. We scan it with both lights, panning away from us to follow this other level's presence to a corner of the wing, where there's an ascending shaft. We approach the shaft from the main floor but can't get a good angle on its exit path. Scanning back along the mezzanine, we are surprised by a metal ladder attached to the stone wall near the arched entry. Against the natural presence of caverns, tunnels, and sinkholes—abraded over millions of years by chemical compounds blended with the force of flowing water—the man-made ladder is strikingly artificial.

"There may be another ladder in that shaft," Pilar says. "But I want to check down here first."

"What are we looking for?" I say.

"Bones or fragments of bones," she says. "Human bones."

She walks to an expanse of shingle, gets down on her haunches, and sifts through pebbles and small rocks. I pick another part of the space and do the same. Ten minutes on, after collecting small fragments, I find what looks to be a leg bone, either femur or tibia, and show it to her. Pilar says it's the former. She's uncovered a large piece of a skull and other assorted bones.

As we're comparing discoveries, spreading them on the ground, we both notice a distant rumble, as if from a far-off thunderstorm observed over a plain or bay. Thinking that's exactly what it is, we resume our sharing, but, snap, the volume jumps to ten thousand majorettes twirling rain sticks indoors. In the moment it takes to stand, a din has erupted, like the reverb of a jackhammer keeping time as a subway express roars by.

Pocketing the bones—I stick the femur in my belt—we climb the ladder to the mezzanine and move toward the ascending shaft, Pilar leading the way.

A geyser of water and detritus belches from the chasmic pit just before an upriver tsunami crashes through, filling the center space with a deluge and breaking onto the mezzanine.

Sloshing along, I slip and fall into the torrent, sinking below the surface. Rising, I wave the flashlight in circles, trying to see Pilar and get my bearings. I find her, light jammed in her belt, back at the ladder, yanking it with both hands.

She frees the ladder, but its weight escapes her grip, the top coming down over me. Although I dodge it, the metal frame grazes the back of my head and scrapes across an arm, shoving me under again.

I rebound, swim to Pilar, and find footing on the mezzanine. The flood pulse, though, has reached my chin, and she's now treading water.

"There's no ladder in the shaft," she says.

That's why she was trying to reposition the ladder that fell over me.

"The water will lift us up," I say.

"I didn't see an exit."

"We'll deal with it."

By the time we get to the shaft, the opening is under water. We dive to get inside the passageway, barely wide enough to contain the two us, back to back. Like juice rising in the straw of a squeezed container, we float upwards, pushed by the force of the flood pulse.

Above, I spot a glimmering circle and point it out to Pilar. We shine our lights in the direction of the glimmer and illuminate what appears to be a hatch. The water continues to rise and us with it.

Having floated up to an arm's length from the exit, I give my light to her and push at the hatch. Then I pound, but it only moves a little.

"I'm going under, to come back up feet first," I say. "To bust through."

"What if it's locked?" she says.

"I'll kick harder," I say. "If that doesn't work, press your face to the hatch and the gaps where the light's coming in. The water will bleed out the same way, and down the hill. A tiny bubble under the hatch should stay clear."

"Unless the hatch is in a sump," she says.

"Whose side are you on?"

I take a breath and submerge, moving below Pilar. Pulling knees to my chest, I turn upside down and extend my feet to the hatch. Hands tight against the walls of the shaft, I flex my legs and kick. There's greater give than when I pounded it with my hand. I kick again. The hatch loosens. I kick once more, and my legs go straight through.

Light fills the space, and I feel Pilar's feet against my legs as she climbs out. I right and hoist myself from the shaft, then join her seated by a side of the exit away from an ongoing flow of water. The hatch did have a padlock, but I see that I managed to split the fixture's single hinge from a wooden base.

"Well, Agent Cruz, you sure know how to show someone a good time."

"Life's full of surprises, Senator," she says, wringing out her vest. "What exactly was that?"

"A flood pulse," I say. "Overflow meets the domino effect, with possible siphon boosts, supercharged by gravity."

"Since we bought ourselves some time, could you try it a little slower?"

"*Some* time?" I say. "How about big time. But to answer your question, internal basins, far up in the mountains, reach overflow. From underground springs, heavy rainfall, groundwater saturation. They spill over, priming the next downstream basin, sinkhole, or pit to do the same."

"That was a tidal wave, not a single domino," she says.

"The sequential flow accumulates and accelerates," I say. "Because of confluence and gravity."

She gives this some thought but, refocusing, gets on her feet and scans the nearby slopes. I notice that rain is still falling. Our clothes will not be drying soon. Where we are is a very small clearing, surrounded by a thicket of dense vegetation and tangled trees in all directions. The way back to the car will be difficult.

"There it is," Pilar says. "PDL's research facility."

She points to a partially obscured white, windowless building, high on the ridge of an adjacent slope. There are no other structures within view, and no visible roads or power lines. Just a block of tofu on a bed of mixed greens. The key to its otherworldly appearance could be that modular components were lowered in place by helicopter. More probably, with all the trees, you just can't see the roads that brought in the builders and their equipment.

The bigger reveal is that Pilar already knows about, or today found online, reports that PDL experimented on bodies at a research center, information I received from Abdul Khan after she left the restaurant. To what extent that activity is a factor in operation Imposing

Encounter I don't yet know, but it's clear that she is fired up by PDL.

"That's why you were looking for bones," I say.

"Yes," she says. "There were inquiries about improper use of bodies, but nothing was found at the research facility."

"It's a long haul from there to here," I say. "Especially without a path."

"Reason is a power," she says, approaching the uphill perimeter of our playpen patch and crouching to peer through undergrowth. "But the ruthless use deceit to traffic in the unreasonable." She inserts an arm into the greenery and holds back a swath of branches. "Look at this."

Ten yards beyond the tangle is a beaten path, wide enough for two, but narrow enough that vegetation creates a canopy, an enclosed arborway.

"The other end's probably masked more," she says. "We'll use the path to reach the road up there and connect back to where the car is. We can check out the facility tomorrow."

WE TAKE turns in the car changing into dry clothes, then drive higher into the mountains to arrive at La Fuente, a one-time coffee estate that is now a parador inn and spa. Besides an original mansion, which today houses a restaurant, there are guest rooms converted from the former casita quarters of farm hands, built by the bank of a river.

Night is falling as we're seated for dinner on the mansion's veranda, the only guests at a facility that enjoys the bulk of its offseason business on weekends. The night manager provides a complimentary bottle of wine, a basket of bread, and menus to peruse, after telling us that the cook has been summoned from her home in the valley. He claims there was a mix-up over whether we'd be dining here this evening, but Pilar says the question wasn't asked when she made the reservation. It may be that the cook is simply running late. Another staff member brings us a cheese board with a generous assortment.

"I could go for some shrimp," I say to Pilar, eyeing the seafood offerings.

"A Wednesday in the mountains might not be the best time," she says. "Although, they may have frozen shrimp."

"An old guy on Martha's Vineyard told me about frozen lobsters coming back to life," I say, turning the page on the menu. "You can't get much fresher than alive. But he didn't mention shrimp."

"Senator, were you alone when you first met Sarita?"

I look up from the menu and see her staring at me from over the rim of her wine glass. Another question. This morning it was my age, then came the one about drinking.

"It was in a restaurant," I say. "Late afternoon. I was alone in a dining area. She was seated at the far end of an adjacent bar. A man was at the other end. Nearer to me. She was nursing a drink. He was surfing his cellphone with one eye on the television. There was a game on. I'm not certain, but he probably had a drink in front of him, too. When I sat down, I chose a seat facing away from both of them. I had no need to intrude on their thoughts. Any other questions?"

"Who introduced her to you?"

"I didn't mean that literally."

"Okay, but who introduced you?"

"No one," I say. "I didn't learn her name until the next day."

"But you did speak with her, right?" she says.

"How do you know that?" I say.

Pilar sucks in her cheeks to deflate what might have become a smile. Intelligence people—as well as intelligent people, in general—often make a face at questions in answer to their questions.

"I don't," she says. "I guessed it since you said this was when you first met."

"Those aren't my words," I say. "She presented herself at my table uninvited, and without an introduction, after posing a rhetorical question to an almost empty room."

"Didn't you find that unusual?"

"Not now," I say. "She posed often and to great purpose, as we've already discussed."

She puts down her glass and glances away, as if considering a retort. Her holding back tells me she understands she can't push our dialogue for details without reciprocating, which she's under orders to avoid.

"It looks like our chef has arrived," she says.

A woman has gotten out of a car in a parking lot on the other side of the river from the hotel grounds. She crosses a footbridge and treads a path toward the back of the mansion, carrying, but not opening, an umbrella, for the rain has stopped.

"Your powers of perception are as sharp as your spelunking," I say. "Hopefully, the end results won't threaten our lives."

"I'll test your food, if you're worried," she says, eyes wide but without a smile.

The chef's driver emerges from the car and lights a cigarette, standing under a lamp. Taking a drag, he exhales a momentous puff, worthy of a signal or a ritual. But something else has gotten Pilar's attention.

"Did you hear that?" she says. "It was a coqui."

Focused on the smoking driver, I had not noticed the distinctive call, ko-kée, from one of Puerto Rico's famous tree frogs.

"It came from over here," she says, lowering her voice and pointing to a bush brushing up against the veranda railing beside our table.

As if cued by her index finger, the coqui shoots from the bush and lands within the fringes of another plant.

"Wow," she says. "That's a once in a lifetime event. You never see them."

"And it's after we swam in water flowing underground," I say. "Not your same old same old."

"They say the coqui can't survive off the island," she says, still staring in the direction of the coqui's disappearance. "Perhaps that's what happened to Sarita."

This blend of whimsy and ironic empathy is a side of Agent Cruz I've not seen before. The moment passes.

"Earlier today, you mentioned the work we've chosen," she says. "Why did you go into politics, Senator?"

At least it's off topic.

"After the academy, I was given ship assignments and then two years in naval intelligence. As much as I liked sailing the seven seas, and valued security analysis, I wanted to serve our country at the ground level."

"Why?"

"People pursuing their lives justified, without daily assaults on their dignity, that's where you find community. Out of that dynamic comes consensus for positive change."

"How did you start?"

"As a teenager I had volunteered for one of Senator Sam Jacobs' reelection campaigns. Then, during summers when I was in law school, I worked for him as an intern in Washington. Once I earned my law degree, I got a job as an outreach coordinator at his Providence office."

"Doing what?"

"Engaging with a diverse range of community constituents and stakeholders," I say. "And representing the senator at local events."

"Good experience at corralling consensus," she says.

"Great lessons for a learner," I say. "Spurs and bits."

"What was the first position you ran for?" she says.

"Mayor of Woonsocket, a small city," I say. "It didn't hurt that my great-grandfather had once held the position and was well remembered."

I remind myself that while the name connection was a decided benefit, not all familial ties to the city stir the soul. My forebears moved to Woonsocket from Québec in the 1860s, earned money recruiting French-Canadians for textile mills, bought land, built housing for the workers, and got rich. The enclave grew, sprouting churches and parochial schools, with all subjects taught in French as late as the 1920s. The rich, now mill owners themselves, exerted old world control over working class brethren in the name of protecting their culture. Certain sons of the rich—though not the daughters—learned English in private secondary schools and studied law, the better to exercise legal defenses against assimilation, as well as unions. In 1928 lay leaders opposed a call by the diocesan bishop, an Irish American, for English to be used in all Catholic high schools. The dissidents withheld funds for the bishop from their parishes, dissed Irish Americans in a bigoted newspaper, and sued the bishop in civil court. The ringleaders, including in-laws and associates of my family, were found guilty of insubordination and excommunicated by the pope. Then gradually the Depression hit, and suddenly the mills closed. The rich became less different.

"He was very well remembered," I say again, leaving the negative thoughts unmentioned.

"Deep roots are usually a strength," Pilar says. "Unless someone poisons the groundwater."

Another assertion giving way to irony, per the added twist of an apparent mind reader. But those are stories for another day.

"After serving as mayor, you went to congress," she says. "For two terms."

"Facts are so much easier than questions," I say.

"But not closer to the truth," she says. "What was all that fuss about when you ran for the senate? If you don't mind my asking."

"Mind? The free bottle let me off easy. Imagine the Q and A we'd be having just to order wine."

"I guess it's none of my business."

"I'm a senator, and you're a citizen," I say. "It's totally your business. Senator Sam Jacobs died near the end of his fifth term, four months before election day. Party leaders and the governor pushed his widow, Vivian Perske, to run in his place."

"She's your chief of staff."

"Who's telling this story? The opposing candidate, Kieran McCluskey, was campaigning as a change agent. Reversion was a better word. He highlighted the months Sam Jacobs had given to cancer treatments and argued that Rhode Island deserved a fulltime senator. Vivian had dealt with health issues of her own. She thought someone should run who could negate McCluskey's strongest point and continue Sam's legacy."

"You didn't request her endorsement?"

"No."

"But you didn't turn your back on it either," she says.

"No, I did not."

"So, a woman presents herself to you, out of the blue, with a question of whether you'll take the place of her husband, and you say yes," she says, eyes wide open.

"The awful truth," I say, prospecting for humor. "No one had to tackle me running away."

"It fits a pattern," she says, without a comic edge.

"How so?"

"Your ties to women," she says. "With all due respect, Senator."

She has deftly brought us back on topic.

"No one enters life but through a woman," I say, which gives her pause. She smooths a wrinkle in the tablecloth.

"Of course, it's not as if you were sitting on the fence teasing for her support," she says. "At least not from the accounts I've read."

"I didn't have to. Two former governors were old themselves. The other congressman—Rhode Island only has two—was already running to replace the current governor. That left me. As for Sarita, she did all the teasing."

"Isn't that what men always say?"

"Being senator doesn't make you a tower of strength," I say. "In many ways, you're just a tower. A dumb monument. But if there's any pattern to my life, it's that I've learned much from women who show strength of purpose."

"To women who serve without lying down," she says, raising her glass.

Pilar takes a long sip of wine, the bowl and base of the glass blocking a view of her eyes. She may feel she's put a period on the conversation, but I have questions of my own.

"What brought you to counterintelligence?" I say, once she's lowered the glass.

"I started my life at the bureau in the Criminal Investigative Division, CID, on teams surveilling and interdicting narcotics traffickers," she says.

"Catching drug dealers," I say.

"Trying to catch drug dealers," she says. "Not always successful, but I respected that the mission was organized. There was structure, like fighting a just war."

"When the action's justified, commitment follows."

"To a point," she says. "I was committed enough to go undercover, once I saw what inside info could do."

I'm shocked to hear this, picturing a range of abuses that

undercover work in the drug trade might mean for a woman.

"The risks in that world must have been all-in," I say, concern surely showing on my face.

"I was set up as a bulk purchaser, with my own crew, all FBI people," she says, reacting to my misapprehension of absolute danger with a wry look. "I wasn't embedded, in any sense."

"Okay, then," I say. "The worst that could've happened is you might have been killed. That's not so bad."

"Not as bad as what drove me out of CID."

"Which was?"

"The death of innocents," she says. "Transnational shippers and urban distributors use violence against women and children for acts of enforcement or revenge. Even worse, they inspire stringers, peripheral hoods, juiced wannabees, who kill more randomly. They do it to stake a territory, a market. Their gunplay promotes drive-bys and shootouts, with innocent lives mowed down like extras in a video game."

"You've witnessed it," I say.

"The aftermath," she says. "A toddler's head blown clear off by fire from an automatic weapon. Another time, a kid's face unrecognizable from the mushrooming of a hollow point bullet. This other time, I ran to a little girl lying on the floor next to a knocked-over chair. Her eyes were open, looking at me. But when I reached her, I saw her severed arm under the chair in a pool of red. She had bled to death."

"There are no answers," I say. "None that right the wrong."

"We have so little time to make a difference," she says. "After years of arresting criminals—doing my part—I decided that locking up more bad guys wouldn't get me to a future. Or help create a future I'd like to see. I wanted to do something worthwhile."

"Counterintelligence."

Pilar lowers her voice to just above a whisper. Deep feeling speaks through her eyes, as well, more affirming than assertive.

"Keeping our democracy safe and functioning is the best way to bring about change, to take the American experiment to eleven. Someday the moments we've waited for will come."

"Did anything else inform your choice?"

"I'm old enough to have seen the parameters of possibility stretch for women and girls. STEM careers, leadership roles. We have to keep leaning on the corral gate, get it to bend wider to let more heifer calves poke their way out. Push positives to overcome the horrors."

"Where do you see yourself?"

"In a place where the faces aren't looking through me."

CHAPTER 11

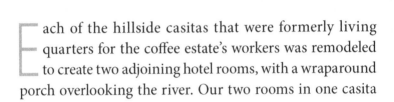

Each of the hillside casitas that were formerly living quarters for the coffee estate's workers was remodeled to create two adjoining hotel rooms, with a wraparound porch overlooking the river. Our two rooms in one casita are connected by a lockable door.

Before going to bed, I shut off the lights and stand by a window to take in the setting. Upriver, moonlight catches froth from a waterfall, with the stream churning chop as it flows by the casita. I'm contented to end this day watching the river flow and not be worried about it.

From a side window I spot the chef and her driver on the veranda of the mansion. He's pouring her a glass of something. Each has a cigarette in their other hand. Time to celebrate, having schlepped up this mountain so we could have dinner.

There's an open-faced ceramic oven in the room, with coals still glowing. A hospitality card on the dresser offers delivery of more coals, as needed. I turn the existing ones over with a poker and stir up sparks. They'll be fine. I don't even feel a chill.

Head on the pillow, I'm asleep almost immediately. Later—I have no idea of the time—knocks on the door snap me awake. The knocker repeats a staccato triple rap, successively softer. My consciousness clears, and I remember where I am. Out of bed, I make sure the chain is locked and open the door a crack.

It's the chef, asking me in a low voice if I need more coals. She's holding a lidded bucket, tongs attached, with an oven mitt. I don't need coals, but she's made the effort, so I let her in.

I neglect to turn on a light. But our eyes are adjusted to the dark, and this shouldn't take long. Flickering embers lead her to the oven, and she transfers a dozen coals from the bucket. Wielding the poker like a wand, she arouses a glow, then turns to me. Light from the oven illuminates her face.

"I can heat the bed," she says, putting down the poker.

Her eyes are glassy. Likely because she's had a very long day.

"No, the linen might catch fire," I say, so wiped out that I'm seriously thinking she means coals on a tray under the bed.

"No fire," she says, reaching out to touch my arm. "Me."

Looking down to follow her touch, my eyes now wide open, I notice in her other hand, slack at her side, a shiny object reflecting orange light from the coals. It's a knife.

I grab her forearm above the knife and twist. She slaps across my face and scratches my neck, then kicks at my groin but misses, as I fend off thrusts with my free hand. Digging a thumb into her wrist, I twist some more, then spin around, banging the knife hand against the dresser.

The knife pops out and away, skittering into the shadows of a corner. I let go of the chef and hit the floor, slapping my hands on the surface to find the knife in the dark.

Something slams the abutting wall in Pilar's room, halting my search and sending a framed picture crashing, broken glass tinkling off key, like a wind chime in a hurricane. I resume groping for the knife, but the chef whacks my back with the poker.

Up on my feet and challenging her, I parry slashes and yank the poker from her grip. As I smack the chef with my palm, the door from Pilar's room bursts open. She tumbles through, hanging on to the chef's driver, who's wielding a knife of his own. While Pilar has both hands around his wrist below the knife, he's flailing away at her torso with his other hand.

I pounce on the driver's punching arm and whack him on the chin. Before I can pound him again, the chef slits the back of my thigh. Turning and slipping off him, I find her standing over me with a piece of broken glass, glinting fire from the oven. I kick with both legs, knocking her down, but the driver frees his knife hand from Pilar and rolls on top of me.

One of my hands is punching his face, while the other holds tight to the arm brandishing a knife. A stab spikes the floorboards by my ear, and I slide my grip to his wrist to keep the blade impaled, our free hands parrying in a duel of fists. The guy lands a kidney punch, then sits up and rocks his torso to loosen my grip on the knife hand. I roll aside and raise a leg as he yanks the blade from the floor for another thrust.

A gunshot lights the space like a flashbulb and silences the room like a gong. Pilar has fired into the ceiling.

The driver is out the back door to the porch. I pick up the poker and race to the front door, the chef fleeing ahead of me. Letting her go, I wait at the ground entrance to the wraparound porch. Having made the porch corner, the driver sees me with the poker blocking the path, does an about-face, runs toward the river, leaps up on a railing, jettisons over the rapids, and completes a death dive into the water, curled tight until plunging hands and feet first. I watch him surface and emerge from the river twenty yards downstream.

"Are you all right?" Pilar says, standing by my side.

"Yes," I say, feeling sticky blood on my thigh. "Just a cut. How about you?"

"I'm fine."

"Do you want to go after them?" I say.

"No. We won't learn anything. They're locals, with no idea why they were asked to do what they did."

The chef has run across the footbridge and jumped into their car, which kicks up gravel as it motorvates out of the lot.

"We could find out who hired them."

"Whoever hired *them* is fringe, either low ranking or out of practice," she says. "They're not in a position to know any more about Imposing Encounter than we do."

"They could know more than me," I say.

"You know quite a bit, Senator," she says, walking back into the room and turning on a light.

Blunt supposition has again entered her voice. I figure since we're not about to go back to bed, this would be a good time to air out her issues, whatever they may be. However, she sees the broad streaks of blood on my leg and returns to her professional self, running up the hill to the mansion for a first aid kit.

While there, she has a discussion with the night manager, a young man listening to music, who is the only other person on the premises. She tells him about the intrusion but limits details of violence, to make plausible a wish to avoid reporting it to the police, not wanting to interrupt our trip. Per Pilar, he relaxed once he understood the police would not be involved, and the only issues to report to his boss would be a dismounted bolt lock and broken glass from a picture frame.

"Minimized problems and an overnight worker's need for company got him to open up," she says. "He told me the chef was a replacement, supposedly a friend or cousin of the regular chef, who called in sick."

"It wouldn't have taken much cash for the regular chef to forgo traveling up a mountain and cooking for just two people," I say. "Even if we are big tippers. Especially when she had no idea what would happen."

"She had to know something bad was going on," she says. "Think about it."

"Then let's arrest her. You're in the FBI."

"Bigger fish to fry, Senator. Bigger fish to fry."

Why does her talking to me sound like she's talking about me? All the same, she assists in applying disinfectant and gauze to my wound, then wrapping a bandage. That done, I help her move the dresser, so she can stand on it to caulk the bullet hole in the ceiling using a bar of soap.

Afterwards, we hike up to the mansion. The night manager had told Pilar he would prepare coffee and put out some fruit, rolls, and cereal. We take our coffee on the veranda and listen to the collective coquis tuning out as dawn approaches. A few hearty members of the choir keep singing beyond sunrise, perhaps aware that soloists get more attention.

Before leaving, we dodge through a brief shower to visit La Fuente's spa center. The largest space is a yoga room lined with photographs of Sarita, both alone and with guests.

"I have something you should see," Pilar says, taking a folded piece of paper from a blouse pocket. "Teodoro showed me this yesterday."

It's a photo, clipped from a newspaper, of Sarita pulling a curtain down from a building sign. She's wearing a ball gown and a tiara. The caption explains that PDL used the occasion of New Year's Eve Y2K to install signage reflecting its new name, PDL Biopharma, refashioned from Ponce de Leon Pharmaceutical.

"She's totally unchanged," I say, in a bass-ackward observation, before correcting myself. "The woman I knew was totally unchanged."

"Did you look at that one?" she says, pointing to a picture in the corner.

Sarita stands in the center, with women on either side, and a half-dozen seated on the floor. Behind them, mounted on a wall, are the words El Encuentro, fashioned from branches and leaves.

"It refers to the 500th anniversary of Columbus," she says. "Use of the term discovery was ditched."

She observes me knotted in a mental calculation.

"She could've been...," I say, not finishing the thought.

"It happens in Hollywood all the time," she says. "Right?"

"The same, only different," I say.

"I'm sure your campaign advisors tell you how popular you are with older women, including seniors."

"The preferred term is advanced."

Outside, under the orange-red blossoms of a flamboyant tree, we find a stone sundial. On its rim a brass plaque reads,

WITH ETERNAL THANKS TO SARITA
ON THE OCCASION OF THE 50TH
ANNIVERSARY OF THE AHL FEDERATION
OF YOGA PRACTITIONERS AND THE 30TH
ANNIVERSARY OF LA FUENTE.

"She definitely had a thing about time," she says.

"Why do you say that?"

"Who puts a sundial under a tree?"

"Rain might tarnish the brass," I say.

"As I see it, questions keep piling up," she says. "Maybe we'll find clues at the research facility."

Pilar walks away. I stare at the sundial, where two birds have landed to drink water captured in the grooves of Roman numerals, from flowers dripping above, doing what they must to live. I kick at pebbles in the sand around the base.

"Enough with the musing, Senator," she says, pivoting to face me with a raised hand. "How many fingers?"

I catch up to her without comment but turn for another look at the sundial.

"It's not like she was *your* mother," Pilar says.

We find the research facility in a state of reconstruction, with a loaded dumpster parked by a boarded-over entrance. While the building sides are windowless like the back, which we saw from the valley below, there are four windows in the front. Three are covered by plywood, but one second-story window is serving as a portal for a chute to the dumpster.

There are no cars or trucks in the parking lot, and we see no signs of anyone present. That being the case, we climb the demolition chute, untie a tarp, enter the building, and turn on lights.

We come across a couple of operating rooms and a bank of fifteen cadaver refrigeration units. Another large room has dozens of tanks of compressed gas, four human-size shallow tubs on wheels, each with multiple faucet connections for external sourcing of fluids, and a walk-in refrigerator containing a series of taps, possibly for ice water. However, the water main has been shut off.

Other rooms have been fully demolished, their dimensions outlined by remnant markings on the floor. We search in vain for an office or filing cabinets. Lastly, Pilar makes a point of inspecting the elevator cab.

We exit and inspect the area around the entrance. Amidst debris beside the front steps, we uncover an encased and locked notice board, in which is posted a form of building permit. I hold the whole thing up so Pilar can take a picture. Then I look closely at the permit. It's mostly boiler plate, with the names and addresses of the general contractor and architect, start and expiry dates, approved work hours, safety provisos, contact numbers, emergency listings, and supervisory designations. What must have drawn her attention is the name of the property owner, QTS Sustenance LLC. There's no reference to PDL. The name sounds vaguely familiar—QTS Sustenance—but I can't place it.

"I'm surprised there aren't any labs," I say, as we get into the car. "At least not among what was left. You'd think a medicinal drug company would have a laboratory."

"There's probably one at the headquarters," she says. "PDL doesn't have many patents. They mostly produce generics under private labels for drugstore chains. The PDL name is used on vitamins and supplements."

She gives me instructions for getting to the mountain town of Utuado, where we'll have lunch and prepare for the teleconference meeting with Badge and Josh.

"Did anything in there surprise you?" I say.

"No. It matches up with what I found online about their handling organ donations. And the complaints."

"So, they had a contract?"

"Yes. Initially, it was for delivering organs removed at hospitals. But disaster situations created operating room delays. PDL got approval to set up their own operating rooms, and they attracted the necessary surgeons."

"Any questions about why their facility was up here in the mountains?" I say.

They argued it was more centrally located than Arecibo or San Juan," she says. "It's also closer to Ponce, the second largest city, on the southern coast. And they bought a helicopter."

That explains why the building stands out so prominently from afar. They cut down trees for safer landings on the roof, a roof accessible by elevator, as Pilar confirmed.

"No wonder people got suspicious," I say. "The bodies were taken to PDL, and the organ removals were done by doctors who worked for them."

"Hospital administrators pointed out that in a disaster or health crisis, when the focus is on keeping people alive, the needs of the dead are secondary."

"Of course," I say. "Except that total control is an invitation to abuse. PDL could hire doctors with past problems, liability issues, and pay them to take out every reusable organ, even if the deceased donor only okayed removal of their eyes."

"That was a major complaint," she says. "And inconsistent paper trails got PDL in trouble."

"What kind of trouble?"

"Med schools received cadavers missing kidneys, without documents."

"Documents?"

"Cadaver transmittal forms were supposed to show approval for any prior procedures," she says. "PDL blamed all errors on the frantic pace of removals during emergencies."

"Sure. And when the frantic pace left a body too defiled to pass on, they disposed of it in the cave pit."

"There was that, and then the rumored experiments," she says. "Something about using chemicals to stabilize bodies for longer organ viability. They would've had to get rid of the failed test cases."

"Where did the rumor come from?"

"A doctor under prosecution for Medicare fraud, hoping to reduce his charges," she says. "He claimed he learned about the tests when he did some procedures for PDL. But he had no evidence, and investigators found nothing."

"Do you have any idea why the building permit is not in the name of PDL?"

"I read that they assigned the government contract to a new company, maybe to insulate PDL from future lawsuits," she says.

"What was the name?"

"QTS Sustenance LLC, the company on the permit."

This organ business, while reeking of criminality, may just be an illicit sideshow to whatever ties, if any, PDL has to operation Imposing Encounter.

"I imagine it's off-topic to the matter at hand," I say. "Correct?"

"I can't comment on that, Senator," she says. "But I'd like to see you bring it up during the video conference."

CHAPTER 12

We find a remote, shady spot in an Utuado parking lot to prepare for the virtual meeting. Pilar positions her laptop on the car's dashboard, to the right, so the camera captures both her, now in the driver's seat, and me, in the backseat. The transmission hookup is via her cellphone.

"If we tell them about last night's assault, they'll insist you return to Washington," she says, turning to look at me.

"I won't go," I say. "I want to revisit PDL and confront the guy who blew us off. He told someone up the line about us and that person told someone else."

"What are you saying?"

"Eventually, a PDL higherup aware of Sarita's role in the scheme—whatever the scheme is—decided to impress his boss by hiring local toughs to take us out, or at least scare us off."

"I never said PDL is directly involved," she says.

"No, you didn't," I say. "But going after two obscure journalists over Sarita says they are."

She turns away without concurring.

"I won't mention the assault," she says.

"I'm not asking you to break protocol with your boss," I say.

"We're all hired hands," she says, staring out a window. "You're the boss."

"Says who?"

"You're elected by the people, Senator," she says, tapping the laptop keyboard to initiate the virtual meeting.

After a minute or so, separate images of Badge Prescott and Josh Kuhn appear on the laptop screen.

"Good afternoon," I say. "I guess Mick Golden's busy today."

"Everyone's busy, Senator," Badge says. "But Mick is tasked with raising the DHS terrorism advisory from a bulletin to an alert. We don't want to do that without specific details. He's on needles and pins."

"Based on what you told me two days ago, there's already enough threat information to issue an alert," I say. "That would be useful for airlines, port security, and border patrol."

"It's not good to double-dip on alerts," Josh says. "We're expecting credible timing and target intel a day in advance. That in hand, DHS will be in position to issue an imminent alert and recommend protective measures."

"Under the circumstances, there's little to be gained with a step one alert," Badge says. "And, as discussed, it might signal we have a source."

"Won't they know that once DHS issues the imminent alert?" I say.

"Our belief is that the action will be in its initial stages when target details are made available," Badge says. "In preparing for the attack—and announcing it as imminent—it would appear that we simply moved quickly in response to ancillary intel's backing of AI analysis."

Their matter-of-fact certitude about the situation exceeds the reach of communications surveillance and AI algorithms. Yet, aside from my own contact with violence, and the recently uncovered revelations involving Sarita and PDL, I've seen no evidence of a threat from operation Imposing Encounter.

"Circling back, would you brief me on the nature of your ancillary intel?"

"It kicks in after we've achieved critical mass with surveillance data," Josh says. "I'll give you a sideline example. Last Friday, I was meeting some friends for dinner in Adams Morgan. I knew we'd be splitting the bill, so I stopped at the closest ATM for cash. The screen indicated that my debit card was inoperable. No reason given. I'm forced to use a credit card to get cash. Later, I call customer service for an explanation."

"And?"

"I usually stop at an ATM in Georgetown, where I live," Josh says. "And I always use my bank, MHT, to avoid a fee. Well, MHT's AI system detected I was in Adams Morgan, not Georgetown, and using another bank's ATM, even though there was an MHT ATM a block away, which I didn't know."

"Customer service gave you ancillary intel," I say.

"They took in the facts and explained what happened," Josh says. "But it was AI that terminated my debit card. We don't have that capability when it comes to terrorists."

"You also don't have any more surety," I say. "Freezing your card was due to an interpretation of data that presumed felonious intent on the part of an imagined thief, where none existed."

"If surveillance tracks align chatter within targeted subsets, we can program guided concentrations on follow-up searches," Josh says. "We can even drill down to the reverse directory level. But you're right—especially since, in this case, we're dealing with the late General Kharrazi's disparate, disconsolate ronin—culpability at the other end of the line is not a given. Direct confirmation is required."

"Who's your ancillary intel source when data from NSA's hundreds of millions of surveilled transmissions shouts out anomalous word couplings, and there's no easy path to explication—like with, say, Crossfire Hurricane—and AI has exhausted multiple sources of exegesis in search of meaning, including the collected works of Shakespeare, Virgil's *Aeneid*, and *The Art Of War* by Sun Tzu?"

"You neglected to cite *Moby Dick*," says Badge. "Closer to home."

"We contact the British, the Germans, the French, the Israelis," Josh says. "If the signifier registers with any of them, we ask if they've sussed out an operative correlation through human intelligence."

"Their human sources are your ancillary intel," I say.

"Yes. They have feet on the ground in certain places where we lack traction. Once we receive an ally's help in forming a construct, data from tightened surveillance begins to cohere. Then we approach our own sources for corroboration."

"That's where Mr. Rashidani of PDL Biopharma comes into the picture," I say.

Pilar sits up and raises a hand, not for permission to speak but to cut me off.

"As I indicated yesterday in requesting the meeting, the senator's information concerning Sarita Montoya uncovered a credible connection to PDL," she says. "Once that was established, he deduced my interest in the company was more than casual. However, I shared nothing about PDL that could not be found online."

"The senator doesn't deduce, he observes," I say.

"Alright, then, Senator, perhaps we should call you Hawk-eye," Badge says. "I can understand, given the start to your week and details newly learned, why you might consider David Rashidani of PDL Biopharma to be involved with Imposing Encounter. Parts of what we're going to disclose will lead you further astray in that regard, but he is not."

"I'm sure I'll be all the wiser for whatever you choose to divulge, Badge."

"David Rashidani started life in Iran as Ali Salman," Badge says. "While a graduate student in biochemistry at UCLA, Mr. Salman was recruited by SAVAK, the Shah's security force, to spy on fellow students in exchange for paying his tuition."

"It's estimated that one out of every ten Iranian graduate students in the US was a spy," says Josh. "The Shah wanted to keep tabs on prospective dissidents."

"SAVAK hoped to curry favor with the bureau by sharing useless bits these student snitches passed on to their handlers," Badge says. "That included the stuff on the Iranians, but, in addition, highlighted any reports on American students in their orbit. Who was smoking pot, who went to protest rallies, who was attending rock festivals where politicians were demonized."

"Isn't that just the sort of thing the bureau was cultivating in those days," I say. "I remember reading that in 1972, when Patricia Schroeder first ran for Congress, the FBI paid a guy to break into her home looking for who knows what, all because she was against the Vietnam War, had very long hair, and wore peasant dresses."

"No comment," Badge says. "What I will say is that we weren't going to start individual files on seventeen members of a UCLA fraternity getting stoned at a Grateful Dead concert. However, I did interview and create a file on Ali Salman himself, who was a relentless source of non-actionable intel. Take it from there, Josh."

"It turned out that Ali Salman was a double agent, in spirit if not in fact," Josh says. "When the Shah was overthrown, he left his job as a research biochemist in Tehran and joined the Revolutionary Guards. Later, as Iran looked to invest oil profits in the US market, he was picked to front an oriental rug business in New York."

"They funded these startups—there were many—through offshore banks as intermediaries, due to the financial restrictions against Iran," Badge says.

"Salman became Rashidani, an Iranian Jew granted asylum in the US," Josh says. "After a few years, he convinced his honchos that a pharmaceutical business had better growth potential than rugs, and PDL was born. In order to funnel him more capital, and to boost his bona fides, the Iranians had Rashidani demand compensation through the Iran-United States Claims Tribunal at The Hague over the expropriation of commercial property in Tehran—a manufacturing plant and a number of warehouses—that supposedly belonged to him."

"They ran into a snag, though," Badge says. "Two of the warehouses had already been cited in the compensation case of another refugee, their rightful owner. Rashidani said it was an address typo, but his entire claim was denied under the general principle that where there's smoke, there's fire. Facing a heavy load, the tribunal seized upon any error to veto a case."

"Central Intelligence had a team monitoring the tribunal," Josh says. "We didn't want righteous advocacy on our side to be sullied by con artists. Questionable claims were referred to the bureau for stateside follow up, including Rashidani's."

"An FBI appointment was made under the guise of possible assistance with the tribunal case," Badge says. "When I walked into Rashidani's office, I knew I had met him before, and I saw in his eyes the same awareness as we shook hands."

"Not a Grateful Dead moment," I say. "But a dual déjà vu's one strange trip."

"Our hands remained gripped for a very long time," Badge says.

"You reached an agreement without speaking."

"Quite," Badge says. "In exchange for our not sharing his FBI-generated, SAVAK-friendly file with his revolutionary associates in Tehran, and accepting that the bureau's eyes would forever be on him, he agreed to cooperate on security matters linked to Iran."

"Yet, you insist Rashidani's not a source concerning the event about to happen."

"To reiterate, his mission involved finance, not espionage," Josh says. "Over the years, he *has* been able to provide input, derived from his ongoing security contacts. He's confirmed the accuracy of certain conclusions drawn from fact or inference, but usually as a tertiary, or more remote, source."

"To be frank, however, as the PDL business grew, his scientific interests took hold, underpinned by entrepreneurial acumen," Badge says. "Rashidani's developed a successful enterprise. At this point, his involvement with Iran has come down to a sharing of profits, not intelligence. And I wouldn't be surprised if his profit-sharing agreement had a sunset clause."

I'm wondering if it's already snowing in DC, because I may need a shovel to expose the agenda behind their words. Badge is touting Rashidani, ostensibly an Iranian operative, as worthy of an award from the Chamber of Commerce. Conversely, there's not a peep about Sarita's link to PDL. I'm mad enough to mention last night's assault, decidedly a response to our inquiry at PDL's HQ, but doing so would put Pilar on the spot for not saying anything earlier.

"Sunset clause?" I say. "Given our sanctions, Iran's under-the-table sponsorship of businesses is more about currency than profits. They need US dollars. That need isn't going away. Meanwhile, a woman on a mission to see if senate intelligence knows of a plot to attack the US is linked to PDL, and you say nothing."

"There are six mosques and Islamic centers in Puerto Rico," Josh says. "General Kharrazi's shadow army of loyalists likely tapped those congregations for participants, who, in turn, pulled the woman in."

"The woman was Rashidani's mistress," I say. "Given all that you've told me, how could plotters use her without him knowing about it?"

"He's had a few mistresses," Badge says. "They keep getting younger, or maybe it seems that way because he's gotten older. Besides, would you deny the woman agency? You thought you knew her pretty well."

"She admitted to obligations that I now believe were about curative care. Things Rashidani and PDL were in a position to address, but not a ragtag bunch of Kharrazi loyalists. In fact, Agent Cruz and I discovered a facility tied to PDL, but owned by an LLC, that was involved in experimental procedures."

Badge had been tapping a pen. He put it down. Josh had been scrolling on his smartphone. He stopped.

"Our first thought was they set up an LLC to deflect liability from PDL over performance lawsuits," I say. "But based on the tenor of today's conversation, I think it has something to do with concealment."

"Concealment of what?" Badge says.

"Purpose, participants, and financial gain," I say. "Do the footnotes to PDL's financial statements list affiliates or related LLCs?"

"Pilar, I'll let you answer that," Badge says.

"PDL's a private company, and the statements aren't audited," she says. "As our analysis has referenced, joint ventures and associated LLCs are cited in the supplemental notes, but without details."

She's directed her comments to Badge. I lean forward from the backseat and catch her eye.

"Did you get information on any of those affiliates?"

She looks at Badge and Josh on the laptop screen, then turns to me.

"Authorization to seek and obtain protected documents concerning those companies was not officially sought," she says. "It was not considered a priority matter."

"Last question," I say. "The LLC named in the building permit at the facility this morning, QTS Sustenance. Was it cited in PDL's financial statements?"

"Not that I recall."

"There you go," I say, facing Badge and Josh. "Hidden from routine review by either Iran or the FBI. Yet, it's a company controlled by Rashidani that may be conducting experimental procedures, about which we know nothing. Agent Cruz found articles about that online."

"I see what you're getting at," Badge says. "However, having monitored them closely for a long time, we have a secure sense of PDL's scope of operation. It's a fuller comprehension than what you'll find in a financial statement."

"I'll grant you that," I say. "But do we know what QTS Sustenance does?"

"I wouldn't imagine that its capabilities represent a threat to the United States," Josh says. "Terrorists aren't known for arranging heart transplants."

"Precisely," Badge says. "You're grasping at straws, Senator. Recent experience is no guarantee of future activity."

He's right. Events of the last few days magnify the dots I'm connecting. An overlap with Imposing Encounter doesn't discount the possibility that my line of reasoning is tangential to the immediate concern.

"Nonetheless, inquiries should be made," I say.

"So they shall," says Badge. "Just keep in mind that what we're facing could be many things. It might turn out to be a mega yacht, loaded to the gills with explosives, piloted into Pearl Harbor to blow up the Pacific fleet. We don't yet know."

"Our informant on the pending threat has delivered accurate intel in other circumstances," Josh says. "His current disclosures cohere with what we've learned from our allies. The hope is, we get word from him, or others, to take out that ship, or whatever it is, just in time."

"He's much younger than Rashidani," Badge says. "The revolutionary patina still shows, and the contacts are fresher. Rashidani, to his credit, has becomes an unrepentant capitalist."

"That doesn't make him a patriot," I say.

"The final word," Badge says. "With that, we have to sign off."

The laptop screen goes black.

CHAPTER 13

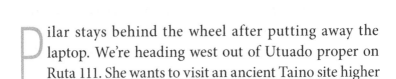

Pilar stays behind the wheel after putting away the laptop. We're heading west out of Utuado proper on Ruta 111. She wants to visit an ancient Taino site higher in the mountains.

The route's inclines become steeper, and the roadway narrows to one lane, a faded solid line down the middle. We enter a sequence of one tight turn after another. She has driven the road before and laughs when I mention hairpin curves. It's the first time I've seen her laugh.

"What's so funny?" I say.

"A friend of mine said this road had more hairpins than a perm."

"No straight line to the horizon, like your Texas," I say. "Speaking of curves, I find it odd that Josh mentioned heart transplants in talking about PDL. I only referred to experimental procedures."

"He must have checked the PDL file after I requested the meeting," she says. "In one case that got attention, a celebrity received a heart they provided. Other people had been waiting longer."

"Fine, maybe he brushed up on PDL, the same PDL I'm being told to ignore," I say. "But then Badge made a point that their informant was much younger than Rashidani and still revolutionary, whereas Rashidani, long ago, had been in the Revolutionary Guards. Comparing the two that way subconsciously linked the informant to Rashidani, bringing us back to PDL."

"You have an overreaching imagination, Senator," she says. "That comparison was between two individuals. PDL wasn't mentioned."

She's a tough nut to crack. But I'm seriously bothered by the casual obfuscation of Badge and Josh. It's more than not disclosing intel. I feel misled.

"Okay, so Josh Kuhn's the director of CIA's Middle East Mission Center," I say. "Does that mean he should know how many mosques there are in Puerto Rico?"

I look at her reaction as I await a response. The eyes show concern. She glances away.

A truck horn blast quells the quandary. A cornering semi springs into view. She yanks the steering wheel to avoid a collision and hits the brakes. We skid to a stop, the right tires surfing dirt, the left leaving rubber.

"Are you all right?" she says.

"Absolutely," I say. "It was my fault. No more questions."

In time, we reach the Caguana Ceremonial Ball Courts Site, built by the Tainos on a highland plateau over seven centuries ago. The courts, called batayes, were used in a ball game played between two teams. The games carried ceremonial meaning beyond competition. Moreover, the layouts of the batayes feature an alignment with certain astronomical movements.

We're too late to tour the museum, but the grounds are open. Some of the batayes are bordered by stone monoliths, most carved with human or animal images. Pilar tells me these petroglyphs are pictorial representations of ancestral spirits, known as zemis. She approaches a monolith and touches the upper edge of the stone as she takes in the image.

Following a separate path through the complex, I come to a grove of trees. I recognize some as mahogany, but there are trees bearing large gourds that I've never seen before. Branches bow under the weight of these green spheres, curving like parentheses around the site's ancient spirits.

I turn to shout out a question about these trees, only to see Pilar, in front of a petroglyph, raising her arms high over her head and slowly spreading her hands wide in a sunrise arc. The question on hold, I continue to explore the grounds.

Finding more unusual trees, my upward focus discovers that the sky has darkened. Across the valley a silent bolt of lightning flashes over another tall peak. Individual rain drops strike nearby leaves. Knowing what's coming, I jog toward the parking lot, getting to the car at the same time as Pilar. A downpour soon hits.

"Were you praying for rain?" I say.

"Why do you say that?"

"I saw you raising up to the old ones."

"Oh," she says. "They may be old, but they're still vital."

As we drive, she tells me that the gourd trees are calabash. Dried shells of the fruit make sturdy bowls and water containers. The smaller gourds are used to fashion maracas.

"And the fruit can be eaten," she says.

"It nourishes many needs," I say.

"Diverse needs," she says.

Hoping that the hard rain will pass, I decide to pull off the road at a restaurant. A pickup truck towing a food cart is poised at the exit, likewise waiting out the storm.

We listen to three songs before the weather begins to clear. A man in a white cowboy hat then gets out of the pickup truck and walks toward us. I lower my window. The man stops and breaks into a grin that aims a footlight at the cloud cover. It's Abdul Khan.

"We meet again," he says. "I'm blessed."

"You're a busy man," I say. "I see you're retrieving one of your carts."

"I call for it, but it does not return," he says, laughing like he's being tickled. "As my British friends say, if the mountain will not come to Mohammed, Mohammed will go to the mountain." He stops laughing. "I could use some assistance, if you wouldn't mind."

"How can we help?" I say.

"Impatient drivers do not appreciate the difficulty of towing a cart down a steep and snaking road," he says. "Would you be my buffer?"

"Certainly. No problem."

Mr. Khan gets back in his truck and heads out onto the road, cart in tow. We follow at a distance of three car lengths.

"Where did he have the food cart?" Pilar says. "I didn't see it at the Caguana site."

"Maybe it was on the other side of the ball courts."

"Where's the vendor?"

"He or she probably lives around here."

"Why not leave the cart at the vendor's place?"

"The vendor may not have a place," I say. "He may be renting a room. Besides, Mr. Khan's probably worried about someone stealing parts. Especially the cooking unit. Like thieves ripping out catalytic converters for resale."

"Possibly," she says. "It's still a very long haul, up and down the mountain every day."

"I forget I'm talking to the FBI," I say. "It's not like he's towing it to Arecibo. I bet he has a garage in downtown Utuado. That's only ten minutes away."

"We'll see."

Khan has to slow down for the first sharp, downhill turn. I brake to create more space. In the rearview mirror I see a car drawing near. We round the bend, and I accelerate to close the gap with Khan, not wanting the trailing car to think of passing.

We're one length behind the food cart when the trailing car hits us. I think it's an accident, but it smashes into us again, this time at the left rear, trying to push us off the road. There's no breakdown lane and no guardrails. The wooded drop-off is steep and deep.

I swerve to the middle of the road, hoping they can't get an angle on us, but in the mirror I see they've moved hard left.

"Look out," Pilar says.

An oncoming car appears, passing Khan's truck. Its horn blares. I veer back to the right. This car streams by and off the road, up the slope.

The trailing car is still banging our tail. Ahead, Khan waves for us to pass him. Seeing no vehicle at the upcoming curve, I steer to the far left, hit the gas, and churn up roadside detritus as we overtake his truck. Once we've passed, he moves to the middle.

Approaching the next turn, Khan slams his brakes. We hear the screech and the skid. In the mirror I see the towed cart jackknife. The trailing car skews right to avoid a collision but clips the rear of the cart and flies into the air. It crashes and explodes at the bottom of a ravine.

We stop, and I back up the car to where Khan is. He's already out of the truck and staring down at the burning vehicle with a vexed look on his face. As I reach his side, I hear him mutter something that sounds like "hay win." His upper lip sneers, and it appears as if he might spit, but he doesn't.

"Did you see anyone get out?" I say.

"Too late for that," he says. "How is your car?"

Khan brushes past me and ignores Pilar as he walks to where we're parked. The license plate took a direct hit, and its frame lost a piece. There are multiple scratches and cracks in the plastic on the left side rear. He bends down to inspect the undercarriage.

"It feels secure," he says, standing after pulling at the bumper components. "You should go now."

"There's no reason for you to handle this yourself," I say. "We'll stay and give a statement."

I want to see how he explains everything to the authorities. Where was he coming from with the cart? A usual spot? Where's the vendor? Pilar was way ahead of me on this.

"You were already helping," he says, managing to present a glimmer of his usual smile as he gestures toward the burning wreck. "Then this fool tried to run you off the road."

"We were involved," I say.

"Involved, yes. But it was my cart he smashed at the end."

Pilar puts a hand on my arm and presses.

"There's nothing we can add to explain why," she says. "He can give the police sufficient facts as to what."

"An intelligent woman," Khan says, as she walks away. "Now I see the journalist."

"I should take notes," I say, squinting my eyes at his.

Back in our car, driving down the winding road, Pilar is tapping on her cellphone. Twice I glance at her and then the phone. She ignores the silent summons.

"He set us up," I say.

She keeps typing, paying me no mind. I wait awhile for her busy thumbs to rest.

"You were right to be suspicious," I say.

Now scrolling, she locates something and takes out a pad and pen.

"See if there's a Bengali word that sounds like hay win," I say. "I heard him say that as he looked down at the crash."

"I doubt he's Bangladeshi," she says, while writing on the pad.

"Does it matter?" I say, deciding to let more time pass.

She pockets the pad and pen, rests the phone in her lap, and stares straight ahead.

"I requested a phone call with Badge Prescott. I expect to hear from him in an hour or so. You can listen in, but I don't want him to know."

"What if I have questions?" I say.

"Appeal to heaven, Senator," she says. "If you can't promise to be quiet, I'll go to a park."

"That's not secure," I say. "I'll bring you back to the caves.

They might be dry by now."

"What's not secure is our situation."

She lowers the seatback, stretches out, and closes her eyes.

RETURNING TO Arecibo, on the north coast, we find a parking lot far from PDL's HQ and Khan's restaurant. Pilar receives a text postponing Badge's call for another thirty minutes. She asks me to get her an ice cream cone, having spotted a Cacique Cream shop across from where we're parked.

We've both finished our cones when Badge's call comes through. I'm already in the backseat and immediately drop out of sight.

"Did the senator complain about not being included?" Badge says.

"No," she says. "He's been good about giving me space when necessary."

"Where's he off to?"

"I sent him on a mission to find ice cream."

The lengths some people will go to, to avoid lying.

"I imagine you've had to put up with a lot of questions," Badge says.

"Yes, but he never pushes," she says. "I tell him nothing, except what he doesn't want to hear."

"Forever the sphinx."

"As I mentioned in my text, I thought I might make better use of my time here investigating the local connections to General Kharrazi that Josh Kuhn hinted at."

"First off, your priority is watching over the senator," he says. "You can't be dragging him along on investigations."

"I could park him at the bureau's office in San Juan."

"Under what pretext? You've seen how he behaves. He'd just walk out. The bigger point is, Josh didn't say the plotters were there. He said they may have used contacts there to obtain the woman's services."

"But why Puerto Rico?" she says. "There are plenty of out-of-work actresses in Manhattan."

"There are some Iraqis and Afghans on the island, with positive memories of Kharrazi, who know about her and would have passed her name to the plotters."

"But you could find more Kharrazi loyalists in New York City," she says. "Including those who fought in Iraqi militias he trained, or with him in Afghanistan when he helped US forces confront the Taliban."

"A key difference," he says. "Kharrazi associates in Puerto Rico would be familiar with the woman's liaison work for PDL's business interests. That knowledge carries an assurance of discretion and trust."

Referring to what Sarita did as liaison work imparts a delicacy that belies the big picture, while simultaneously staining her performance around the edges to obscure a core truth. She was used. While floored at the moment, I have standing to make that case, having been at the center of one such liaison gig.

"An assurance of trust only resonates if the Kharrazi parties know who Rashidani really is," Pilar says. "That presupposes his tie to the plot."

"Don't agree," Badge says. "If open identity contact

occurred, he simply functioned as an informational, not operational, source."

"What about the other thread in my text?" she says. "We should learn more about PDL's affiliates and joint ventures."

"If you're talking about the body parts, they've moved on."

"That's not certain. And if so, we should know what they've moved on to, and where."

"Who cares?" he says. "How could a terrorist hurt us with donated organs?"

"The company the senator cited earlier, QTS Sustenance, may be conducting experimental procedures here in Puerto Rico that could have terrorist applications."

"In what way?"

"Biochemical treatments of unknown use. Potentially lethal. Since we lack info on the company, there's a chance they're not under FDA supervision, like PDL is."

"Don't you think Yosef would've told us?" he says.

A long silence. Perhaps Pilar's concerned that now I have the name of their direct intel, their source, because she let me listen in. More broadly, his outing appears to confirm a link to PDL, although, as with other things, Badge or Josh could say I was reading too much into it. At the very least, it would be tough for them to deny the source's tie to Puerto Rico, given the context of Badge's question.

"We should ask him about it," she says. "And expect an answer."

"Will take it under advisement," Badge says. "Have to go. Give my regards to the senator. Hope he liked his ice cream."

I rise after hearing Pilar slam the dashboard. I see her slam it again.

"Everything okay?" I say.

"You wouldn't understand. People listen to you."

"Not your two friends. They hear me out but pay me no mind."

"Welcome to the club, Senator," she says.

"First thing tomorrow, we contact Badge Prescott and tell him about the road rage incident. We'll say it happened today after your phone call."

"How does that help?"

"If somebody wants to murder us for asking PDL about Sarita, Rashidani must be seriously involved in the upcoming event."

"You heard Badge," she says. "His connection may just be circumstantial. Remember, the same local contacts who led the plotters to Sarita could know other people at PDL."

"You made a case for Rashidani's tie to the plot," I say. "Badge has to lean on him. Use the assault on us to pressure the guy. Compound it with the leverage he's maintained over their long-term relationship and squeeze him for details."

"Doing that will spur what I meant when I said our situation's not secure."

"How so?"

"Stringers will kill you for tracking Sarita's trail and possibly discovering the scheme," she says. "Honchos, if your cover's blown—there were security cameras in the PDL lobby—they'll kill you for already knowing what you know, to prevent a *canceling* of the scheme, for any and all of the reasons they might have."

"What's the difference?" I say. "If they catch up with me, I'll be dead either way, without a doubt."

"Death is the highest form of not secure," she says softly, as if whispering a prayer over a grave.

"Doubtless, without a doubt."

I recall Badge saying it would be better if I stayed dead, so as not to alert the plotters. Leaning on Rashidani for intel about Sarita's involvement would be a red flag, signaling the input of an embedded agent or of a living Senator Tourneur.

"Badge and Josh want the show to go on," I say. "We catch the bad guys in the act and uncover all the connections."

"La verdad," she says. "Put pressure on Rashidani, he smells a rat. The plotters' contacts might pick up the scent."

"A rat named Yosef, I'm thinking."

She does not react.

"As for me, I need to bide my time among the missing, presumed dead," I say.

She turns away and holds her face in her hands.

"I just have to make sure your death remains fictional."

CHAPTER 14

Pilar and I have dinner at a restaurant overlooking Arecibo Harbor. On the advice of our waiter, we share platters of bacalaítos, which are fritters made with codfish, and baked empanadillas filled with ceti, a tiny, seasonal fish indigenous to the waters around Arecibo, together with arroz con gandules.

Regarding a possible itinerary for tomorrow, I tell her I'm willing to dutifully hang out at the FBI office in San Juan. She'd be free to spend her time following up on any pertinent leads from the bureau's local files. That could include a possible meeting with the mysterious Yosef, I say, slipping it in as she savors a piece of bacalaíto.

"Qué será, será," she says, eyes intently revealing nothing.

Pilar wants to stay near the ocean. She finds lodging right on the water in Isabela, four towns west along the north coast. We check in at an office close to the road. Our rooms are in individual cabanas under trees just off the sand. We park the car between the two, the last in a line of a dozen units. The other cabanas appear to be vacant.

Rims of volcanic rock formations have created a natural pool in front of the beach. Waves are splashing against outcroppings on the outer edge of the pool. The tide is out, but the room walls feature photographs of surf and spray erupting over the volcanic rim and inshore rocks at high tide.

As we bid our goodnights, Pilar cautions me not to open the door for anyone. I remind her that since we're at the balmy shore and no longer in the mountains, I won't need hot coals to keep me warm. That said, she warns me to be on guard for any woman bearing lemonade or iced tea. "Qué será, será," I say.

My head's on the pillow, but I can't get to sleep. I'm thinking that Badge Prescott's cool customer routine in the face of an imminent attack would be admirable if it weren't obstinate. Pilar, who must know most, if not all, of what Badge knows, made a reasonable proposal to investigate possible connections on the island. Yet, he dismissed her request as unnecessary, having faith that this Yosef person—the presumptive source—will provide concrete intel at the proper time.

Sweat has condensed behind my neck onto the pillow. I get up and pull back a curtain that shades a glass slider to a patio in front of the cabana. Light from a yellow bulb by the entry teases the space. After opening the slider a few inches, I lower a stopper bar to secure it against further movement. A breeze cuts through the screen, and I hear waves breaking.

Back in bed, I recall the report Pilar cited about PDL using chemicals to stabilize bodies in order to preserve organs. How might such chemicals be applied to mass effect in a lethal fashion? Not being a biochemist and not knowing the actual chemicals involved, this mental exercise is more a jumble than a conundrum. Lacking a rationale, I float a notion that the chemicals draw physiologic energy from inert extremities to keep internal organs vital. *Sleep on it.*

Waking up, likely hours later, my faculties reconvene around the same baseless idea of chemicals tapping bodily energy and immediately discount its potential for terrorism. Not to say, on an entirely different tack, that PDL couldn't produce and deliver toxic dietary supplements to hundreds of thousands.

That potent thought is muffled by the sound of waves crashing closer to shore, a roiling surf pounding the rocks. Lying on my side, I feel the wind powering those waves, with chilled, salt air wafting through the slider screen.

As I tug the top sheet toward my shoulder, I take in a sound that is neither surf nor sea. It could have been a rattle caused by wind, yet the wind's still blowing, and the rattle sounded but once.

Catching a voice, I lift my head off the pillow. There's a man at the slider, skimmed in the yellow light of the exterior lamp, pressing a gun against the screen. A gunshot beats my roll off the bed. I hear two more shots as I scramble to a corner, out of the line of fire.

There's silence and no pain.

"Senator, are you all right?" Pilar says, speaking through the screen.

I exit via the cabana door and join her outside. Abdul Khan is lying faceup on the patio. His eyes are open, with a look of surprise. She kicks a pistol away from his side. He's bleeding from two shots to the chest.

"Are you okay?" I say.

"I told him to drop it," she says, speaking at a low volume. "But he spun around and shot. I had no choice."

She's fully dressed.

"How did you know he'd come?"

"He attached a tracking tag to our car when he inspected the damage."

"When did you find it?"

"While you were getting the ice cream," she says. "That word you heard him say. It means amateur in Arabic."

"And he's the professional."

"Something like that."

She picks up his gun and gives it to me, then holsters her own. Walking around behind Khan's head, she bends down and puts her right index and long fingers to his neck, feeling for a pulse.

"Nothing," she says. "But keep him covered."

She frisks Khan's legs, then checks his pockets, pulling out car keys, a wallet, and a cellphone. Pilar holds the phone over his face to unlock it. Gaining access to his call and text records, she walks across the beach toward the sea, tapping and scrolling. Reaching the water, she pivots, continuing her walk in a wide circle, as she scans the cellphone contents.

Looking through the trees behind the cabanas, I can't make out the office, but a single light shines from its location. If anyone's there, it appears the gunshots didn't wake them. White caps are still crashing at the shoreline, and breakers are launching geysers from among the rocks.

Pilar has stopped walking. She's focused on reading something from the phone. I glance at Khan to make sure he's still dead and see his air of astonishment abiding.

She tucks his phone into one of her cargo pants pockets as she returns, retrieving her own cellphone from another pocket and taking pictures of Khan. Then she closes his eyes.

"We have to hurry," she says, on her haunches and removing his belt.

"I don't think they heard anything at the office," I say.

"That's not the problem," she says. "I reconned earlier. Nobody sleeps there. But we have to secure his body before sunrise."

Pilar rolls the body over and joins the hands behind his back. She pauses, lowering her head for a moment.

"What are you doing?" I say.

"I want him to stay dead," she says.

"Staying dead is my specialty," I say, exchanging Khan's gun for the belt and straddling the body on my knees to bind his wrists.

"I'll go get his truck," she says. "He left it out by the road. Pack your stuff as fast as you can."

By the time Pilar returns, I'm dressed and have finished packing. We put Khan in the backseat of his truck, fastened under a seatbelt. I find his cowboy hat on the floor in the front and place it on his head, pulling the brim down over his face. We wash the patio with wet towels and finish the job with douses of water, tossing the bloodied towels in with him, along with his gun.

I'll drive Khan's truck and follow her lead in our car. She tells me we're going to a pier not far down the coast. We arrive in less than ten minutes. The paved pier extends from a parking lot beside an inlet where small boats are moored.

Per her instructions, I line the truck up at the foot of the pier pointed toward the end, lower all the windows, and shut off the lights. She replaces me in the driver's seat and uses an extension cord, taken from one of the cabanas, to tie the steering wheel in a straightaway position. Putting a rock, the size of a paving stone, by the accelerator—but not against it—she shifts the transmission into drive and gets out.

Pilar tells me to stand ahead of the truck and be ready to slam the driver's side door shut as it goes by. She takes a trimmed tree branch and pushes the rock against the accelerator. The truck shoots forward, and I swipe at the passing door.

Gaining speed, the truck attains sufficient velocity to travel airborne as it leaves the end of the pier, before splashing down. By the time we catch up, running at white caps breaking over the pier, the truck has already sunk beneath the waves.

"This buys some time," she says, turning and walking back toward the parking lot.

I stay focused on the waves, thinking moonlight off the surf might pick up details of the truck, but none appear. As I nod to the finality of it, something bobs out of the froth of a breaker. Khan's white cowboy hat has risen via its large dome of air. It surfs another wave, then flips over and sinks in a tip of the hat.

I jog to rejoin Pilar, who's walking like she has some place to go. "It's good you've got the phone," I say. "His handler or client or whoever will reach out looking for confirmation."

"As time goes by," she says, without breaking stride.

"That's what I meant. Then, we can use that contact to follow up." She doesn't respond, so I add, "To continue investigating, to get to the bottom of it."

"There isn't time for that," she says.

"But we have to keep trying," I say.

"There is no time," she says, now running. She's already opened the door on the driver's side when I reach the car.

"Senator, your bag," she says, pointing.

I look in the designated direction and spot an object on the ground, barely defined in the dark. Walking toward it, I realize one of us must have removed the bag from the truck. *Tourneur, talk about losing your grip.* Message sent, I stop short, remembering I put my bag in the car, not the truck.

The motor's running, and the car's in gear, the tires kicking up gravel as Pilar drives past, headlights off. She loops around the bag and comes back at me, her window down.

"At the road, go right" she says, passing in a counterclockwise circle and leaving me no time to respond.

Making a second loop, she tells me there's a bus stop less than a mile away. On the third circuit, she says I can catch a bus to San Juan. On the fourth, she directs me to check into a hotel and stay there. Lastly, upon completing another round, she promises to meet up with me in a couple of days.

Pilar unfurls her widdershins course and drives toward the road in darkness. Her brakes flash red eyes before headlights fill the horizon, following a right turn.

won't be angry at someone who saved my life, despite having gone off without explanation. Rather, I'm concerned for Pilar's own safety. She couldn't have gotten any sleep tonight, preparing to confront Khan. Now she's on a mission alone. Abandoning me and my potential assistance—on top of leaving me without security—means there must be significant risk attached to whatever she's doing. And because she wants to keep me out of it for my own good, I'm in no position to help.

Reaching the bus stop, I find there are actually two, one on each side of the road. Not far beyond is a strip mall. I sit on a bench at the stop heading east, toward San Juan, and sift through thoughts about where Pilar may have headed, backed by a constant chorus of coquis.

I can't help but think it involves Yosef, the contact Badge mentioned in the last call. While not definite, he could be the source that Badge and Josh are placing so much reliance on. They have described that source as younger and more revolutionary than PDL's Rashidani. But, in this instance, more revolutionary may simply be a tag for someone with more recent links to the Iranian government. After all, as Rashidani has aged, it makes sense his handlers would've sent over a younger guy to eventually take the reins of the substantial cash cow that is PDL. It's just as possible that this individual—drawn to the temptations of wealth inherent in his position—became susceptible to overtures from US intelligence operatives.

A beep on my burner phone interrupts the cogitation. Vivian Perske, my chief of staff, has sent a text: "Inquiries made yesterday as discussed."

I call her immediately.

"Thank you," she says.

I hold back on a deflecting "No problem," sensing a weight behind her words.

"Are you all right?" I say.

"I'm okay. I called the inns on Block Island and Martha's Vineyard, then spoke with Hannah Curley in Providence, who, of course, had nothing to share."

"Good. I appreciate it."

"I didn't contact the state police until the afternoon." She spoke slowly, as if responding under interrogation.

"That's fine. It'd be natural to think it over before taking that step."

"Not for me, Nate. And you know it. I figured it fit with your request."

No one in the office but Vivian ever calls me Nate. Only rarely and never in front of others. The last time she had said my name with such concern was when my wife, Libbie, died.

"What happened, Vivian?" I said.

"We had a visitor. In the office. He insisted he was a longtime friend of yours. Audrey at the front desk told him you were away for the recess, but he deluged her with facts and names from your time at St. Margaret's. Kept pressing to know if you might be back in a day or two. She called me, and I went out to meet him."

"What was his name?"

"He said he was Steve Boyd."

"There was no Steve Boyd at St. Margaret."

"Surprise, surprise. Once I introduced myself as your chief of staff, he lowered the emergency to simmer and turned on the charm. So sorry to interrupt, thanks so much for stepping out, very grateful for your time, the senator and I go way back, in the same Cub Scout den together, only need five minutes. After making a point of staring off into space, I invited him to my office with a low voice and a curt hand gesture."

"How did it go?"

"Before I was seated, he had already rattled off the names of Jack Callahan, Liam Tyrone, and Rob O'Halloran. I know them from your hyper CV. And I remember meeting Liam. He read the recognition in my eyes. Then he extended greetings from another scout in your den, his best friend, Will Welch, in Los Angeles. This guy did his homework."

"It wasn't too hard. Two years ago, I mentioned Jack, Liam, Rob, and Will in a piece I wrote honoring Sister Mary Jonah for the Sisters of Mercy newsletter."

"He brought her up too. Something about movies. She apparently inspired Will Welch to become a film director."

"I take some credit for that. I'm the one who convinced her to assign movies for homework in the fourth grade, and she let me give film reviews in front of the class."

Vivian laughed.

"You should consider a career switch," she said, with a slighter laugh. "I mean, if this incognito mission drags on too long, or you find yourself playing out the string, maybe you raise your hand to lower the ante. Tell them you'd rather be in pictures. Or whatever. I don't know what I'm saying. It's very early."

Silence intruded as I tried to sense what had happened during the remainder of her meeting with Steve Boyd. Something stressed her.

"He must have asked you things."

"A few times he said he was in Washington for only two more days, although he might be able to stretch it to three. He's scouting acquisitions for a real estate investment trust, looking at shopping malls in Maryland. So, he wants to know if there's a chance you'll be back in two or three days. Each time he stated the phrase—two or three days—he tightened himself in the chair and leaned forward. The relaxed reunion guy, waving arms and grinning, was subsumed in focus. Although I kept shifting my gaze around the room, signaling impatience and counting down to his exit, the last time he says two or three days, I catch his eyes drilling me."

"How did you respond?"

"I remember you told me these people think you're dead, and all they need to confirm is that you're still dead. But part of me is worried you haven't explained everything, and maybe your life remains in danger. That worry is in my voice when I tell him I know you'll be back on the job by the end of recess. Next week. That's all I'm sure of, I say. I'm thinking how Sam in remission would swear he couldn't leave this life until he had drawn from himself all he had to give. That, too, was in my voice."

No life would have been long enough for Senator Sam Jacobs to share all he had to give. But the treasure of his being lives on, even as the void in Vivian's world grows larger.

"There's nothing more you could've said to convey what they were hoping to find," I say. "A perception that my location and existence were in doubt, despite your official words to the contrary. My deepest thanks, Vivian. But I'm very sorry for the ordeal."

"It's only trying," she says. "Sometimes, what's needed gets done. By the way, this Steve Boyd did give me his hotel and room number, in case you returned early. However, I imagine we're willing to let one terrorist rep go free to avoid sending the wrong signal. A signal he'd be waiting for, although not likely in that room."

Vivian Perske's intelligence never lets go. In an effort to keep up, I think to mention QTS Sustenance LLC, PDL Biopharma's affiliate, asking her to initiate a staff review of the past year's senate committee transcripts for any references.

"It has nothing to do with my current situation," I say, lying. "The company was cited in a recent article on health care fraud, and it rang a bell. Testimony at some hearing. I've been meaning to check into it."

My hope is that the impromptu nature of this request will calm her fears about my status. Besides, something may turn up, as I've heard the name before, but not from an article. In closing, she lets me know that the Rhode Island state police got back to her late yesterday, affirming a vacant trail and absence of leads. She'll be contacting the coast guard this morning.

"So far, all the inquiries have been low key, with no sense of urgency," she says. "And I'll ask the coast guard to keep their search quiet, to the extent possible. But there'll be leaks. You know that."

"No worries. It's the Friday of Columbus Day weekend. Sketchy, word-of-mouth mentions of a rumored search for a late-returning senator, surfacing Saturday evening or Sunday, won't generate much coverage. Just enough to confirm the impression you gave Mr. Boyd."

THE SUN rose while I spoke to Vivian. Some cars and a few trucks pass, with activity in both directions, but no buses. While my stop doesn't have a posted schedule, there appears to be one on the other side of the road. Crossing, I find schedules for buses going both ways, including a western route to one of the island's other airports, Rafael Hernandez International.

Pilar, among her parting words, said she'd rejoin me in a couple of days. If she's gone to meet with Yosef, the mystery man, on the island, she wouldn't necessarily need two days. But a roundtrip to Mexico would likely require it. I recall Abdul Khan, alone with me in his restaurant—after Pilar's emotional exit—disclosing that PDL has facilities in Mexico and that in recent years Rashidani has spent most of his time there. Yosef, as well? With nothing to do in San Juan, it's worth using my time to try and catch up with her, whether I'm wanted or not.

In the nearby strip mall, I withdraw cash from a bank ATM and get back to the stop before the scheduled airport bus arrives. The trip to the passenger terminal is less than a half hour.

I imagine that Pilar—whatever flight she's taking—is already in the secure area for ticketed passengers. Seeing a group of young people waiting to clear security, I request from them the favor of an online search regarding PDL Biopharma in Mexico, making up that I left my smartphone in checked luggage. They confirm offices for PDL in the Yucatan Peninsula, at a location between Cancún and Mérida.

Finding there's a flight to Mérida in the afternoon and one to Cancún leaving soon, I figure she'll be on the latter, since time is of the essence. As Jamie Boone, using my FBI-provided IDs, I purchase a ticket to Cancún, tapping my genuine debit card for payment without perusal.

Passing through security, I walk a corridor toward the flight gate, sunglasses on, scanning retail outlets along the way but not spotting Pilar. I stop and survey the boarding area from a distance. It's not filled to capacity. A number of seats are loaded with carryon luggage. Off to one side, away from the window and its view of the runway, I discover Pilar, veiled in the shade of a corner. Proceeding in her direction, and trying to think of something clever, I pull up again when I realize she's asleep.

Her face is alert with concern, lips slightly pursed, eyes taut, as if focused on a thought behind closed lids. In contrast, her sunken torso, slouched shoulders, and contracted limbs are curled, a body surrendered to the satisfaction of slumber.

Pilar was up all night, with little sleep the night before, expecting and planning for a violent confrontation and its possible aftermath, all in the cause of protecting me. At the same time, she's working to detect and prevent an attack on the United States, and having to deal with the petulant disregard of superiors ready to snub anyone with the audacity to question their views.

Put another way, she's staying the course of a material counterintelligence investigation, as her bosses maintain a circus-act array of suppositions balanced by conjecture, held aloft via a miasma of possible self-interest masquerading as collective virtue. All the while, she needs to navigate the minefield of a situation where different parties want me dead for similar reasons, tempered by varied expectations, the complexity of which may have deepened through info she found on an assassin's phone. Duty prevails despite her lack of trust in the direction of leadership.

Should Pilar wake now in my presence, that same sense of duty will have her insist on staying, to keep me from going. So I retreat out of sight, remaining within earshot of any boarding instructions.

My seat range is the last to be called. On board, I walk down the aisle, bag raised high, seemingly in deference to people still fiddling to put things away, though really to mask my face from Pilar. Settled by a window, I put the bag on the floor in front of me and peek forward through headrests to see if I attracted her attention. I don't know where she's seated, but she's not in pursuit, at least not of me.

As THE plane touches down in Cancún, I'm thinking Pilar checked her bag—no guns allowed in carryon—and will have to wait to claim it. Not needing to rush to catch up with her, I remain ensconced in my seat behind an inflight magazine, comfortably returning to the mysteries and thrills of Chichén Itzá, while those ahead experience the tedium of deplaning.

So it is that I approach her in the luggage retrieval area just as her bag pops off the conveyor belt onto the carousel.

"Let me get that," I say. "You're carrying enough already."

CHAPTER 16

When Pilar doesn't even try to convince me to go back to Puerto Rico, I get the message that she's on the trail of a link to operation Imposing Encounter and won't end the chase because of me. She denies she's meeting with Yosef, the mystery contact, and refuses to say it has anything to do with Abdul Khan. But the assassin's phone is the only Rosetta stone we have. I sense she's self-consciously downplaying Khan, to brush off the danger he posed and suppress thoughts of future risks to my well-being—not that I'm worried—while miffed I've made that an issue by following her to Mexico.

We ride in a van to downtown Cancún, visit a bank to get pesos from its ATM, and head over to the bus station, where we catch a second class bus going west. Pilar wants to keep a low profile, so we're traveling without air conditioning on a bus that makes many stops. She does let me know that later we'll be meeting with an archeologist, who has served as eyes and ears for US intelligence.

At the third stop a boy, about seven or eight years old, boards with a music box and starts singing to instrumental tracks from the front of the bus. Pilar explains that he's performing corridos, heartfelt ballads of strife, adventure, and longing. In a final song, he repeatedly refers to "mi mujer"—"my woman"—which generates laughter throughout the bus and a raucous round of applause at the end, as the kid mines the aisle for tips before exiting.

"So, what was that?" I say. "The last one, about Margarita. He was definitely sad at the end."

"Sad and hurt," she says. "A young guy gives up everything for a much older woman. Leaves home, leaves school. Gives the woman all the love and attention she craves. When he's not entertaining her, he's a constant audience. Then he complains to her that his life's upended, he's lost his bearings. Wakes one morning, she's gone. His search never ends, yet his heart will always be with Margarita. You know the feeling, Senator."

"My heart's right here," I say, tapping my chest.

"That was mean," she says, with a glance out the window. "I've been rough on you. Judged you. At first I felt you were sincere when you pushed to go to Puerto Rico, to follow up on her story. Except she turned out to be someone I'd heard about in my oversight of PDL. Legendary, and not in a good way."

"How did that reflect on me?"

"I put you in a box with other men. Given the age difference, I got cynical, thinking there's no chance you could've fallen for her. She was attractive and available action, so you took advantage, used her. Maybe hoping for a younger sister in PR. Seeing that as a moral failing, it colored my view of how you snapped the bait, let yourself be played."

"The last part's true, though I gave nothing away."

"Exactly. And who am I to be making moral judgments? I read an old article that said she always 'popped' in soap operas. If that's the case on a small screen, how much bigger the pop must've been in person."

I think of Sarita's smile, but the events of the past three days have chilled the warmth from its memory.

"It takes two," I say.

"As with many things," she says, blue notes in her voice.

Pilar adjusts the seatback and shifts sideways, searching for sleep. I replay what she said in a repeating loop, but her words aren't sheep. A quarter hour of dwelling on her comments leaves me awake. I'm still awake when the bus blows a tire, swerves, and comes to a stop in a cornfield, knocking down three dozen stalks in the process.

After inspecting the blown tire and calling for backup, the driver invites passengers to exit as we await a replacement bus, since the outdoor breezes are cooler than the stationary interior. There's an apron of grass between the road and the maize, with enough room for everyone to claim a space and camp out. Pilar lies down to continue napping, her bag a pillow.

Antsy in anticipation of so much I don't yet know, I sit upright on the grass, observing farm workers harvesting corn on a hill beyond the field. It's a team effort, with some receiving the bagged ears from the pickers and conveying them to trucks, to be driven away by others. The process appears timeless, essential, and fulfilling, an unbroken circle.

An elderly man in a broad-brimmed straw hat and over-sized Wesleyan tee shirt steps into my view on stretched limbs. He's holding a forked stick, a prong in each hand, as he moves slowly forward in extended, knee-bending steps. He turns toward Pilar as if led by the singular end of the stick. Approaching, he looks in my direction and nods her way, the stick dipping. I raise a finger to my lips to signal quiet and care.

"She's a dowser," he says, just above a whisper. "There are water signs all over her."

Pilar wakes up, sees the old gentleman, and stares at me for an explanation.

"His rod bent to the divine in your presence," I say. "Nothing to be afraid of. Water is the source of life."

"Precisely," he says. "Are you here for the cenotes?"

It's my turn to mime a question, shrugging shoulders at Pilar.

"You mean wells?" she says, raising her eyes to him.

"Most certainly," he says, crouching, then settling to a seated position in front of us. "Wells, underground pools of water, deep caverns with streams, flooded sinkholes, subterranean cascades. All of them."

"No, thanks," I say. "I've already been baptized."

The gentleman frowns at me as if I'm a nincompoop and looks to her for an explanation.

"We recently explored caves in Puerto Rico," she says.

"But that's not a reason," he says, taking off his hat and dusting the ground. "Don't tell me you're worried about the bodies? That was months ago. They haven't found any recently."

"What bodies?" she says, sitting up.

"Mutilated bodies were discovered in deep caves, in the water," he says. "Near Dzamal and Tulmo, west of here."

"Were they murdered?" I say.

"Who knows?" he says. "They weren't suicides. They were naked and cut up. Livers, kidneys, and hearts were missing. Even eyes."

"There must have been an investigation," she says.

"I imagine so, but after a while, they didn't cover much of it on television. Other things happened that were bigger news. That's how I know they didn't find more bodies. It would've been on TV."

The man expounds at length on all the gifts, wonders, and imaginings we'll miss if we don't commit to exploring Yucatan's caves, naming a half dozen sites. My mind is fixed on the bodies he mentioned, imagining a connection to what Pilar and I found in Puerto Rico.

The replacement bus arrives, and we reboard, bidding best wishes to our dowsing acquaintance, who chooses to sit at the front, while we take seats among empty back rows.

"Sounds like PDL's sideline activity may be thriving in Mexico," I say, as Pilar scrolls through her phone. "Check to see if there's a listing for QTS Sustenance."

"I will, but I need to read something first," she says.

I glance over a couple of times as she scans a long message. She puts the phone on her lap and leans against the headrest, staring forward. After a minute, she turns toward me with a level gaze and holds it. I notice, give it a moment, and nod.

"Trust me," I say.

"A friend at the bureau responded to a text I sent from the plane," she says, speaking low and narrowing the space between us. "Thirty years ago, Abdul Khan was a member of the Badr Alliance, a Shia Iraqi military group in opposition to Saddam Hussein. Their Iranian liaison for funding and weapons supply was Javad Kharrazi before he was a general. Fast forward to the US-Iraq war. Khan got work with the occupation forces. First as an adviser for local security and procurement and then as a frontline contact with Shia militias. His case for admission to the US was referred by the top CIA officer in Baghdad at the time, Josh Kuhn."

She takes a breath and exhales slowly, having openly shared intel and awaiting my reaction.

"Should I call Josh now to tell him we're still alive?" I say.

"It's more complicated," she says. "Khan's phone shows that Tuesday night, when we flew to San Juan, he received an incoming call routed via a dormant number, to mask the caller's identity. He received another call from that number just before noon on Wednesday."

"After we met with the marketing guy at PDL."

"Right. And just five minutes later, on Wednesday, Khan gets a call through PDL's main number in Mexico."

"So, *somebody*—not necessarily Josh—contacted Khan on Tuesday to see if he was still in the hitman business," I say. "Then again on Wednesday to let Khan know to expect a call from a third party looking to book his services."

"Yes," she says, our heads almost touching, like client and counsel in a courtroom. "Putting aside the connection of Josh and Khan, the big reveal is that someone at PDL Mexico, in all likelihood, ordered the hit. Which confirms your suspicion that they must be involved in the imminent attack. Like you said, why else target two journalists?"

"It's tough to ignore the Kuhn and Khan tag team," I say.

"Block it out," she says, pulling back. "I'm in Mexico because of what was on Khan's phone. Period. To see what's happening at PDL and report back. We can deal with the mystery caller later."

"We can't disregard their prior relationship," I say. "It ties a high ranking CIA officer to a national security threat."

"What about Khan's Kharrazi link?" she says. "The unknown caller could be one of the plotters."

"Why would they call him Tuesday night before we had asked any questions?"

"Because they hadn't been able to confirm you were dead. You might suddenly surface, as you did, and go to Puerto Rico—or have someone else go—in search of Sarita's connections. They were proactively preparing for anyone asking PDL about Sarita."

My jump to conclusion about Josh lacks both hard evidence and overt motive. Her view at least reflects motive. That's not to say my suspicion doesn't linger.

"A tad convenient that their man was in Arecibo," I say. "Josh found out we were driving to PDL's headquarters when you scheduled the virtual conference. How would the bad guys have known?"

"Josh didn't know that Tuesday night, when Khan received the first call," she says. "But the terrorists were worried that Sarita's trail would lead searchers to PDL. Think about it."

Before Wednesday, Josh had no known basis for seeking out Khan purely because of his proximity to the PDL HQ. The plotters did.

"They reviewed their recruitment roster for the best-positioned contact willing to do dirty work," I say. "I get it. So, when do we reconnoiter PDL's Mexican facilities?"

"After we see Brew Peña."

"Your archeologist friend."

"She's more than a friend, she's a mentor. Brewster Warren Peña. She uncovered a number of ancient Mayan sites. I've read her books."

"How can she help us today?"

"Brew's what we call a coupon. Her father, Antonio Warren Peña, was CIA, serving under nonofficial cover during the Cold War. He worked through a front business in Hong Kong. She dedicated a book to him."

"So, she knows the life, is superintelligent, and keeps her ear to the ground."

"And she shares when asked," Pilar says. "I first learned about her during a vacation in Massachusetts. She spoke at a museum in Plymouth run by the Pilgrim lineage society, making her case that the Maya had a culture as complex as those of ancient Egypt, China, and the Mediterranean world. It was a transformational experience. The cherry on top is she's a Latina descended from not one, but two Mayflower families."

AFTER CHECKING into a hotel, we meet Brew Peña in the town of Zotzlam, not far from a buried and overgrown archeological site she and a team came across two years ago. They are currently camped there to mark and map out the locations of evident pyramids, buildings, courts, and terraces, in advance of excavation.

She tells us that PDL's Mexican subsidiary, PDL Bio-pharma, S.A. de C.V., has a solid reputation in the region as an employer, as well as a corporate sponsor of public parks and youth programs. Although neither she nor Pilar has found a reference to QTS Sustenance, either online or through local sources, Brew reports that PDL does have an established program to purchase cadavers. The program is promoted throughout the state of Yucatan, including its capital, Mérida, via hospitals and clinics.

As for the discovery of mutilated bodies in underground rivers and pools, she discloses that investigators identified each one through DNA. They traced them back to certain towns and villages that were hit hard by a hurricane in early June. It caused massive mudslides that killed hundreds and made thousands homeless.

"The destruction was so horrific," Brew says, "they had to bring in rescue crews from neighboring states, Campeche and Quintana Roo. In the confusion, some sketchy characters may have delivered bodies to unscrupulous doctors or clinics that used them for pending transplants and a big payoff."

"Did the investigators look into PDL?" I say.

"They concluded that since PDL has a legitimate cadaver program, they wouldn't deal with questionable sources, Jamie," she says, addressing me by my cover name.

"Based on what we found in Puerto Rico, PDL leveraged authorized access to cadavers to remove body parts," Pilar says. "There's a range of time frames for various organs that allow viable transplant. PDL may have developed treatments or processes that stretched those time frames. They could make much more money marketing viable body parts than selling cadavers to med schools. Vertical integration."

"They may have abused their authority under the Mexican cadaver program in the same way," I say. "Are their facilities close to the caves where the bodies were found?"

"They're in the area," Brew says. "But the underground river may have moved the bodies. Forensic pinpointing of the watery grave into which they were initially committed would be near impossible."

"Having heard us out, is there anything odd or unusual involving PDL and its operations—in whatever sense—that's come to your attention?" Pilar says.

"I've spent my life questioning acts and intentions thousands of years old," Brew says. "I can see you're not here to assist on a local case of mutilated corpses."

"We'll willingly share whatever we find that would help solve that case," Pilar says.

"A non-denial denial," says Brew.

"While our inquiry goes beyond the boundaries of Yucatan, it is equally involved in matters of life and death," Pilar says, looking her mentor straight in the eye. "Nothing would be too small to aid in what we're investigating."

Brew leans back, the better to include the both of us in her gaze.

"One of our crew overheard talk at a bar about bodies being brought back to life at PDL. Resurrection. You can't get more vertically integrated than that."

CHAPTER 17

Drew Peña's mention of dead people rising reminds me of the old guy on Martha's Vineyard and his revived lobsters. Moreover, it's of a piece with reports Pilar found of PDL experiments to stabilize bodies for subsequent procedures and my nagging notions about QTS Sustenance. Before traveling to PDL's Mexican facilities, I reach out to one of my elementary school friends, Jack Callahan, now a partner in a Minnesota law practice, after Pilar locates his office number online.

It's late Friday afternoon, but Jack promises to have a paralegal do a nationwide state records search of established LLCs and report back with whatever they can find on QTS. Jack accepts the mission without knowing the purpose or questioning my need for secrecy.

Pilar and I catch a minibus in front of our hotel that takes us to a town near PDL's production plant and offices. We stop for some food, then set out on foot in the early evening. Approaching our destination, we pause on a rise to view the landscape.

The production plant sits at the bottom of a valley, with a parking lot adjacent to the road. A two-story office building is attached to the plant by a glassed-in passageway. On the far side of those buildings is another parking lot, beyond which is a grove of trees taking up more space than the production plant. The grove thins out to an open area that includes three other buildings.

Overlooking those three buildings, but separated by an additional stand of trees, is a manor house perched on a bluff. To the east, cultivated fields border the entire PDL footprint. Although dusk is settling around us, the northwest sky still bears twilight. Against that horizon, a distant Mayan pyramid touches the clouds.

"If we run into anyone, I'll do the talking," Pilar says, flashing her gun to me, secure and unseen in a shoulder holster under a cotton top. "It's for defensive purposes. We're not looking to engage."

"Understood."

"Say nothing. Remember, we're here to look for signs of activity. We may not find anything, or anyone with answers, but at least we're trying."

"Why don't you contact Yosef first," I say. "I know you don't like me bringing him up, but this would be a good time for an update."

"I haven't heard from him this week. He hasn't responded to my texts."

"Why didn't you tell Badge yesterday?"

"He knows. He's copied on all texts between me and Yosef. Now stay behind me and follow my lead."

With that, she pulls down her cap visor, pivots in descent, and proceeds down the hill toward the crop fields that border PDL.

So, their major source, to some extent embedded

with the plotters—"Along those lines," Josh Kuhn had said—has gone silent, leaving the terrorist attack's zero hour unknown. He may himself be in danger, but no one seems worried except Pilar. That's the real reason we're in Mexico.

Badge's indifference, during yesterday's phone call, to her suggestion of the plotters' presence in Puerto Rico was capped by cold calculation as to Yosef's status. His summary question—"Don't you think Yosef would've told us?"—ignored the man's recent silence and the possibility that his identity as a double agent may have been blown. Thus, her anger at the end of the call, serving as kindling to the fire Abdul Khan's phone records ignited last night. Evidence of Rashidani and company engaging an assassin introduced lethal violence into her immediate fears for Yosef.

As we enter the fields beside PDL, we pass a young boy singing a corrido for exiting workers, accompanied by a girl on guitar. I leave him a healthy tip, tossing cash onto a cloth by their feet. There must have been dollars mixed in with my pesos because the guitarist bows twice.

After walking two hundred yards among beanstalks, Pilar turns left and heads for the three PDL buildings beyond the grove of trees. Approaching from within the grove, we see that one of the buildings is fully lighted and occupied, men in green scrubs hustling to-and-fro among operating rooms. Another building, marked as a research lab, has a couple of lights on but no obvious activity. The third building has only a few windows, and they're all dark. The three structures form a U around a courtyard, opening up toward the gated manor on the bluff above.

Finding a back door to the dark building unlocked, we enter with care and silence and approach the front lobby. It's dimly lit by courtyard lamps through plate glass windows that frame the entrance. Air conditioning has brought condensation to the outside of these windows, blurring our view.

Pilar gestures to a room off the lobby. "Maybe we can open a window in there."

The room is darker than the hallway because its windows are shaded. There appear to be banks of filing cabinet drawers along the far wall and the wall to our left, away from the courtyard. Its center space is filled with what could be desks.

I raise the blind over one of the windows, also fogged up but now allowing light, and feel for a latch. Before I can open it, Pilar taps me on the shoulder. I turn to see tables bearing bodies under sheets, big toes tagged, or in zipped bags. We stand in silence, surveying the room from one end to the other. Stunning as it is to be among so many dead, I notice an anomaly. Before I can say anything or investigate, light moves across the space, projecting our silhouetted heads against a wall of refrigeration lockers, then disappearing.

We duck and peek out at a passenger van stopping in front of the next-door building, the one with operating rooms. Trusting that reflected glare kept anyone from spotting us, I crack open a window for a clearer view. Seven men exit the van. Six are dressed identically in black pants and pullovers and appear to be in their twenties or thirties. The seventh man is older. They are welcomed at a respectful distance by a bunch in green scrubs. A few others rush to join the reception committee from the research lab, crowding the front steps. The black-clad men and their minder recoil a bit, forming a phalanx as they advance, greeters peeling off to grant full access to the entryway. Once the newcomers and their green posse are inside, we hear nothing but the neutral sounds of nature.

"It appears that PDL's involvement is no longer an open question," Pilar says, not to me but to herself.

"The only question I have is why is that cadaver wearing shoes?" I say, pointing to a body a few tables away.

I said it rhetorically, but Pilar's curiosity is piqued. The PDL eureka moment prompts another adventure of discovery. She goes to the shoes, stands by the corpse for a moment, then lifts the sheet above the ankles. As she tilts her head to look, a leg kicks her arm, the sheet rains over her, and a man jumps off the table.

Hearing keys scratch the metal tabletop as his leg kicked Pilar, I make for the door, but with eyes fixed on their scrum. My defenseman instincts are to deny access to the gate. He twists her in the sheet, pushes her to the floor, and rushes to the exit. I crouch to engage, stick my head in his gut, slide it to the side, stop, lift, and throw him down. My knee's pressed to his solar plexus when Pilar approaches, casting off the sheet.

"How are you doing?" I say.

"Never been kicked by a ghost before," she says. "I'm all right. You?"

"One lone man on a dead man's chest. Yo-ho-ho, and a bottle of rum."

Pilar levels her pistol at the fleet-footed phantom, and I release my hold. She begins to quiz him in Spanish as he gets to his feet. After a couple of non-threatening questions, he volunteers that he's a groundskeeper, and his name is Juanito.

At the end of days spent in the sun, he enjoys cooling off before starting a very long commute, naming four villages that he passes on a trek home, walking to save money. He claims there's never been any nighttime activity among los muertos. Until now.

In response to her question, Juanito says he knows Yosef and was around him earlier in the day. Even in the dim light I can see her face brighten. When he agrees to deliver a message at her request, Pilar rips a scrap of notepaper from a pocketed pad and writes a few words. She gives Juanito the note, together with some cash, and instructs him to speak with Yosef in private.

"We'll confirm he's secure, then leave," she says after Juanito's gone, the two of us standing by a window.

"I hope he can share what those men in black are about," I say.

"Destination and objective may still be concealed."

"True. But why the stop here to meet and greet PDL's men in green? Is it a makeover, or something worse?"

She's looking out the window, but with my last question, her focus turns inward, her mien sours. Have I conjured up bad vibes from a past experience with PDL or Rashidani?

"They're coming," she says, snapping out of the funk.

Juanito is returning in the company of our man Yosef, whose steps across the courtyard are measured and sure. The outline of a gun shifts in his pants pocket with each step. The two enter the front lobby and make their way into the morgue without turning on lights.

"Yosef," she says, clasping his arm. "I'm happy to see you."

"Pilar," he says. "This is not good. What are you doing here?"

"We hadn't heard from you," she says. "I was concerned."

"But why are you here?" he says.

"Following up on leads."

"What leads?" he says. Then, looking at me, "Wait. Are you the two reporters that visited the offices in Arecibo?" His feet are now dancing an anxious two-step, pivoting between Pilar and me.

"Yes," she says. "If you're safe, secure, we'll call it a day and go home. But you haven't been responding lately."

"You have to understand, the people that are here—you may have seen them—they react badly to breaches in security. Very badly. They were told about the reporters."

"Who told them?" she says.

"They have contacts in Puerto Rico," he says.

"Do you know these contacts?"

"Me? No. But this guy under contract to do something about it has a big mouth."

"How did you find that out?" she says.

"He gave away details to people he recruited, or tried to recruit."

Nothing yet about the call from PDL Mexico to Abdul Khan.

"Who gave you that information?" she says, her voice rising to a challenge.

"They did."

"Who exactly, Yosef?" she says, seeing that he's equivocating and upset that she ever worried about his welfare. "Flesh it out for me."

Yosef stops moving his feet. I sense that he, knowing the truth and knowing her, has tracked the laser beam of her inquiry and is now calculating his options. I'm still aware of the gun in Yosef's pocket and concerned about his potential reaction to being cornered. Accordingly, I break my promise to remain silent.

"Considering the larger issues, as well as the lethal potential of your visitors, we'll just vamoose at this point," I say.

"Excuse me?" he says. "What did you say?"

"We're leaving," I say, eyeballing Pilar. "Vamonos.

"What do I tell the others?" he says. "Those that saw Juanito hand me a message."

"You're an intelligence agent," I say. "Make up something. Your sister stopped by to remind you about her birthday lunch tomorrow."

"Would my sister pull a gun on someone?" he says, removing the pistol from his pants pocket. "A detail Juanito mentioned."

"I doubt those men in black understand Spanish," Pilar says.

"Maybe not," he says, pointing the pistol at her. "But their commander spent time in Cuba. Give me your gun."

"We're allies."

"We're associates," he says. "Bottom line, it's a business arrangement."

"We share more trust than that."

"Less, actually, but enough that I'm still trying to save your life," he says. "Give me the gun."

She holds her ground and squints her eyes in a glare. He raises his pistol to my head.

"Don't try anything," he says. "Your friend will be dead before you get the gun out of the holster."

"You'll be next," she says. "It's unlashed."

"Maybe you'll be lucky," Yosef says. "Either way, he dies."

Pilar raises both hands, then uses one to slowly pull back her top to reveal the weapon. She removes it from the holster and presents it to Yosef handle first. He steps back, keeping us covered with both guns.

"Take off your clothes," he says. "Strip down to your underwear. Hurry up."

As we undress, Yosef gives instructions in Spanish to Juanito, who proceeds to search the room, lifting up random sheets. The only thing I understand is a repeated reference to a young woman. We're down to our skivvies by the time Juanito finds the requested body.

"Help him carry her over here," Yosef says, addressing me and nodding toward a corner. "Use that chair."

There's a chair with wheels by a desk. I roll it to Juanito, and together we move the female corpse off the table into the chair and bring it to Yosef. He has us dress the body with Pilar's clothes and place it on a stationary chair, then repeat the routine featuring a male corpse and my clothes.

With Juanito at his side, he directs Pilar and me to raise the deceased woman to her feet, each of us lifting under an armpit. Yosef shoots her in the chest using his gun and carries out the same procedure with the clothed dead man, telling us to lay the desecrated bodies on the floor.

Next, he turns to Juanito, who's taking it in like an off-the-rails rave. Using Pilar's gun, Yosef fires a bullet into the young man's forehead, his loose frame folding like a Chinese lantern, then places that gun by the supine woman's right hand.

"He saw too much," Yosef says. "Hurry up."

Pointing to a supply rack, he tells us to quickly wrap ourselves in sheets for warmth. He pulls open two refrigerated lockers on the double and bids us to lie down inside with a wave of his gun. Saying he'll return at some point, he shoves the lockers closed with a warning to keep quiet.

Feeling around the inside front of the locker, I find no latch or handle. Why would I? The dead don't exit on their own. Within a few minutes of our confinement, I hear a muffled sound of voices in conversation but can't make out any dialogue. A half hour along, the interchange is sporadic and projects lower volume, eventually trailing off into silence.

Later, in our joint solitude, I pick up echoes of smothered sobs escaping from the space beside me. I know Pilar's not crying for herself or out of fear. She's crying for Juanito. Moment to moment, I've seen her eyes convey much—savvy, vigilance, valor—without sweat. There's no room for revulsion.

CHAPTER 18

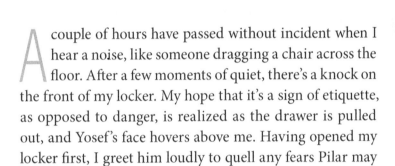

A couple of hours have passed without incident when I hear a noise, like someone dragging a chair across the floor. After a few moments of quiet, there's a knock on the front of my locker. My hope that it's a sign of etiquette, as opposed to danger, is realized as the drawer is pulled out, and Yosef's face hovers above me. Having opened my locker first, I greet him loudly to quell any fears Pilar may have, as he taps and yanks open hers. I rush to climb out and assist but find she's already on her toes, a steely look commanding the room.

Another man, pistol in hand, stands at ease by the door of the now lighted morgue. The cadavers previously lying on tables are all gone. Yosef hands us green scrubs and huaraches. Unfolding the pants and top, Pilar notices the other man staring at her undressed self. She tilts forward on one leg, places a hand on the opposite hip, throws back her shoulders, and challenges him with a curse. Yosef upbraids the guy, whose name is Pedro, then mentions that a dinner has been prepared, as we don the scrubs.

We're outside and crossing the courtyard before he speaks again, to tell us that the visitors have left. Nearing a staircase to the manor on the bluff, we pass a carriage house that is much older than the PDL buildings. My guess is the entire property, including the cultivated fields, was once a grand hacienda, bringing to mind a world of de la Vegas and Zavalas, which I only know from movies.

Inside the manor Yosef guides us to a dining room and invites Pilar to sit at one end of the table, as he and I take seats on the sides. The leering Pedro adjourns to a chair in an alcove, hidden behind a plant. Glasses of water have already been poured at each place setting, with a full pitcher left on the table. I down my water in a long gulp.

"You don't have to hurry," a male voice says. "You'll get a meal, too."

A figure catches up to the voice and smacks me on the back, so hard that I feel the impact of a ring. The man passes and pulls out a chair at the head of the table. I see Whittaker, Walt Whittaker—the lobster man from the Vineyard—taking a seat. But, of course, he must be David Rashidani, CEO of PDL Biopharma.

"I almost didn't recognize you without your cane," I say.

"How the flesh reasserts itself," he says. "I had taken a nasty fall from a rental bike. The diameter of the wheels was greater than I was used to, causing a wobbling sensation. Hit the brakes too hard and scraped my ankle. Everything's fine now."

"Glad to hear it," I say, glaring at the tablecloth, blown away that this guy was directly involved from the beginning, despite Badge Prescott's assertion to the contrary.

"I need to correct that," he says. "My ankle's fine now."

Rashidani makes a show of raising his glass toward Pilar.

"Here's to the welcome return of Miss Cruz to our table and—how should I put this—the surprise live appearance of Senator Tourneur."

Yosef taps his water glass with a table knife, then wields it in my direction.

"That *is* a surprise," he says, an uncanny look on his face. "We weren't introduced."

"Yes, yes," Rashidani says, turning to me. "I understand you again dodged death earlier this evening. You, who questioned my ability to revive lobsters, somehow manages to come back from the brink of demise, time and again. Although I hear Miss Cruz had a lot to do with it. Tonight, that is."

"That's not entirely fair, Doctor," she says. "I must share credit with Yosef. Still, I have seen the senator squeeze out of some tight spots."

Tight and wet, before the hot coals and sharp edges. Then I escaped Abdul Khan's gun with more than a little help from my friend. But her jaunty presence is a shock. My heart picks up that she's reading the room and trying to lift the mood. Except my head is fixed on the emerging hard facts of a conspiracy. I have to dig.

"My first brush with death came after I was tricked," I say. "Why did you choose me to con?"

"You were a willing and active participant," he says. "The correct word is seduced. No one held a gun to your head in Edgartown."

"I was enticed to devious ends, acting in good faith. Your people were playing dirty with innocent lives."

Pilar gets up from her seat, takes the water pitcher, and refills my glass, but generally maintains eye contact with Rashidani.

"Dr. Rashidani, please understand," she says. "The senator is losing sight of the big picture. Not just the need to enable elements of the plot in order to control it, but the greater good to come from the byproduct of your science."

What science? What is she talking about? The moment is interrupted by the appearance of two women with trays bearing bowls of soup.

"He annoys me," says Rashidani to Pilar. "But I promised him a meal, and here it comes. Sopa de lima."

The served dish consists of carved turkey breast in a chicken broth melded with an abundance of lime juice, and garnished with slices of lime, cut strips of tortillas, lightly fried, and cilantro.

"Senator, while you partake of this local delicacy—Yucatan is known for its limes—I'll expand on Miss Cruz's astute observation," Rashidani says. "The science of human longevity forms the core of my research. Accept a short briefing as a capping off of our hospitality."

"I'm listening," I say. Let him talk. The food will taste better hot.

"Identifying and utilizing proteins in young blood can counteract the aging process by replacing damaged cells. Flexibility is restored to the flesh, and organ function is revitalized."

"Hear, hear," I say, reaching for a warm tortilla from a covered basket.

"Separately, increasing the level of NAD, a key molecule, reverses the effects of aging in the circulatory system. After earlier test phases, we've initiated clinical trials for FDA approval of a compound providing both. We call it gyravenal."

"Good luck," I say. "Let's not forget, though, that your ability to conduct research, as well as make profits and find ways to funnel dollars to Iran, exists under an agreement to supply intelligence to the US."

"It's true that my operation involves making money, some of which is shared with others," Rashidani says. "However, financial matters are my least concern. Yosef, here, recently obtained warehouse space to better control all-in fulfillment costs to a major retailer. I never would have thought of it. Yosef, tell him where the warehouse is."

Interrupted mid sip, Yosef puts down the spoon and applies a napkin to his lips.

"Woonsocket, Rhode Island," he says.

"See," Rashidani says. "If such a thing were on my radar years ago, when you were mayor there, we might have broken bread, as he did with the city's economic development team. But incrementally improving profit margins is insignificant to me."

"That's your call, wistful regrets included," I say. "On the matter at hand, however, we expect intelligence, owed under a longstanding reciprocal deal."

"Ever the essentially ugly but not so quiet American," Rashidani says.

I place both hands on the table and level my eyes at Rashidani, preparing to respond, but Pilar cuts the line.

"Doctor, visceral experience has forced blinders on the senator," she says. "His deep focus stares past the give and take that marks our work."

Feeling I'm at the UN, and she's my translator, I take the hint to vacate the Vineyard and stick to the future.

"It's in the interest of all of us that intel be shared to prevent the loss of life from Imposing Encounter," I say.

"Fine," Rashidani says. "Just keep in mind that impertinence is a great leveler, in a negative sense."

"There are worse things," I say, as I parse figurative meanings of leveler.

"Certainly, including deceit," he says. "Let me conclude my briefing on what you should have understood as a report of intelligence. Significant as gyravenal is to the long-term extension of life, our separate research into cryptobiosis, and related pragmatic clinical trials involving suspended animation, are contributing new tools for recouping lives challenged by trauma or disease."

"That's extraordinary, Doctor," Pilar says. "You don't need me to tell you the value of such work in the advance of science and in service to humanity."

"Thank you, Pilar," he says. "Since silence is golden in your profession, I'm humbled by your words, while welcoming more. At the same time, so much depends upon the fall of hair on a woman's shoulder. Wouldn't you agree?"

"Not when I'm eating soup, but it deserves a clinical trial," she says.

"Yes," he says. "Most definitely."

I'm reminded of Badge Prescott's comment that Rashidani has had a few mistresses. After a fortnight of stressed days in the lab, maybe that's his prescription for tension headaches, where others might opt for a long sail.

"I doubt those six men in black were undergoing rejuvenation treatment," I say.

"The men you saw were technicians being introduced to our suspended animation procedures and systems," he says. "Put on operating tables for educational purposes."

"Yosef implied they were dangerous and prone to violence if crossed," I say.

Yosef has forked a large piece of turkey from his sopa de lima but delays putting it in his mouth.

"You misunderstood me," Yosef says.

"Then why did you kill Juanito?" I say.

He chews his turkey and slowly pours himself some water.

"Remember, Tourneur," says Rashidani. "Any agreement we have to provide information, to the extent we have any to share, is with Badge Prescott or his representative, Miss Cruz."

"Let's call him now," I say. "You can fill him in on your overdue update about Imposing Encounter."

"Overdue according to whom?" Rashidani says.

"Me. Because I'm thinking it's possible you and your labs produced a lethal contagion to infect those men in black, who are now on their way to large auditoriums in the US to cough up a plague."

"Your conjecture is so unfounded as to deny hypothesis," Rashidani says. "You want to talk lethal? Five days ago, someone I knew well for a long time was still alive. Not a perfect person. One of her faults was relentless pursuit of a physical ideal, with too many cosmetic surgeries and a couple of elective transplants. It got to the point—as a film director famous for the seamless flow of his movies once said—I could only see the seams. Yet years of pleasure lay ahead of her. She was always seeking to draw life from new wells, to absorb vitality into her being. But now she's dead."

"I'm not the one who sent Sarita on an espionage mission," I say.

"No, you're the person who killed her," he says.

"That wasn't my intention."

"I'm not her father," he says. "Don't speak to me of your intentions. Sarita had good intentions, too. Before gyravenal she benefited from earlier anti-aging treatments. To give back, she volunteered to undergo suspended animation, completing twenty-four hours in total. Four of those hours were just last month, after which she celebrated adding an entire day to her lifespan. But the process—inducing a state where metabolic activity is depressed, like hibernation—is not without strain, especially for older adults. Beyond that, she had exercised and dieted to reduce her body fat to nine percent, which, as I advised, could compromise the functioning of her heart. She didn't listen and paid the price. You were the angel of death, but the ferryman was Badge Prescott."

"Why are you blaming Badge?" I say.

"The friends of Kharrazi wanted verification that the US was clueless as to their plot. They suggested a sting on a member of the senate intelligence committee. I conferred with Prescott, and he offered the names of four potential marks, seen as easy setups. You, ninety-three-year-old Tuck Wheedley, Lester Tatertowne, who speaks in syllables, and one other."

"John Ronson," Yosef says. "A cheesehead, inside and out."

"Exactly," Rashidani says. "Prescott guessed Sarita might be involved and, if so, figured she'd have some say on the man of the moment. He rigged the options in your favor. That was an act of deceit."

There's a bassline overload in his tone and cadence pushing the grievance. Having revealed a covert tie in acting with Badge to aid the plotters, Rashidani's wrath suggests a previous deceit may have twisted their relationship. I'm thinking infidelity, a thought prompted by Badge's coughing reaction to my report of Sarita's death, as we sat in the conference room at FBI headquarters. An onion layer for a later time.

"Hold on," I say. "I'll accept for now that the men in black were just transient medical technicians. Yet you just disclosed conferring with the plotters, who, although they're intelligence operatives, somehow needed help in getting the names of senators on the intel committee. On top of that, they apparently approached you, as Sarita's talent agent, to sign her up for the gig. Not only does that make you an accomplice, it's also the polar opposite of what I got from Badge Prescott. His kiddy version was that Yosef here—without naming him or describing his position at PDL—had a vague tie to the plot, close enough to confirm certain particulars, and to be at possible risk, but was not involved in something like a sting on a US senator. So, what gives?"

"Tourneur," Pilar says. "You can't expect everything to stay within the lines."

I don't. And why is she getting personal all of a sudden?

"You have to accept that the origins of the plot are amorphous," she says. "They're sui generis, rising up from disparate components, cell leaders acting out of their own particular attachment to Kharrazi. A top-down model of a director setting the field and calling the shots doesn't apply. The ordered event emerges from a dissonant, chaotic concoction."

"There's a bigger dissonance," I say. "Neither Rashidani nor Badge has voiced the harmony of when and where the attack will happen. Badge is highly secretive. Holds expectations hostage. Doesn't show all he knows. Won't move on evidence."

"You're confusing containment with inaction, Tourneur," she says.

"Sure, I'm confused. You and I experienced attacks and witnessed lethal violence, including on the grounds of this hacienda. Rashidani conspires with terrorists—purportedly assisted by US intelligence—which ends up with Sarita dead and people trying to kill me. What is it all about? Just sound and fury signifying nothing, or sassafras and molasses covering up something else?"

"This isn't C-SPAN," she says, dripping with scorn. "An observant man knows when to hang fire, including words."

A week of narrow escapes has me in no mood to listen. It's set me loose. I turn to Rashidani, who doesn't appear to have touched his sopa de lima. The spoon still sits on a napkin, but his eyes reveal hunger.

"The readiness is all," I say to Rashidani. "And I'm ready for answers."

"Tourneur, this is Mexico," Rashidani says. "Your moldy toga gets you nothing here. I've told you more than I had to because it is without consequence. So much for your inquiry. I hope you enjoyed Puerto Rico."

"The ultimate question I have—"

"I'm ready for that clinical trial, Doctor," Pilar says, cutting me off, both her hands hitting the table with a solid smack as she rises. She walks along the other side of the table toward Rashidani, an arm moving to the play of her torso. Getting up, the doctor takes her hand and leads her away.

I move to follow but the barrel of a gun presses my back. Leering Pedro has emerged from his alcove post.

CHAPTER 19

Yosef and Pedro escort me to an apartment on the second floor of the nearby carriage house and jail me via a padlocked chain through a wrought iron gate. All the windows are barred. And there is no attic or ventilation system to crawl out through. I observe the two men walk back up the stairs to the manor.

A half hour later I hear activity in the garage below and then the starting of a car engine. Looking out over the driveway separating the carriage house from the staircase to the manor, I see Yosef at the wheel of a car, exiting the property.

It's a clear night. My attention shifts from the array of stars to a torchlit terrace extending from the manor. A breeze caresses the flames in unison. I open the window to catch the air. Moments from this evening flicker in a searching replay. Then I see the evening is not over.

Pilar and Rashidani appear on the terrace. She's in a strapless gown, her hair down upon her shoulders. Balancing a champagne flute, she sways in broad turns around the space. On and off, her movement stops, and she's framed between torches, her head tilted. I don't believe she's listening to Rashidani's words—if so I can't hear them—rather, she's taking in the moment. Or setting it up.

Having roamed, Pilar sits on the thigh-high terrace parapet. She downs the contents of the flute and puts it aside, stretching arms behind in support, hair cascading as she leans back. Rashidani stands in front, probably talking, but who knows. He may just be casting a spell. They walk off the terrace together, leaving the empty flute behind.

Tired though I am, it's not a dream. I lie on the bed, struggling to order the events of the day, starting with Abdul Khan prowling at the slider door. Late images of Pilar keep flashing out of order, playing tricks and adding discord to the narrative. I can't deny an ire of feeling cast aside. Trying to defy what I've seen is like drinking a gin and tonic to quell anger. Rage ensues. Fever courses my lips as I conk out.

I WAKE to meandering voices. Farm workers are passing the carriage house on an alternative way to the fields, having walked in from the main road. It's Saturday, so there are children among them. No day off for anyone when crops need to be harvested. Saturdays as a kid, I'd leap from bed past Remington portraits of cavalry officers and Native Americans and a lithograph of the USS *Constitution* and head out on adventures, exploring a suburban mansion under construction or biking with Jack Callahan to the firefighter school to watch them put out flames. The only work I had to do was selling Cub Scout raffle tickets once a year.

I look up at the terrace, atop a sheer stone bulwark twenty feet high, itself built upon an outcropping of rock. The empty champagne flute has been removed, and in its stead there's a coffee mug. The crown and brim of a straw hat peak above the parapet. Imagining Pilar on a chaise lounge, I pull up a chair to await the next scene change.

The parade of workers has ended by the time she stands, book in hand, to take in the terrain through sunglasses, a dressing gown draping her presence. Her focus is on the fields beyond, not the carriage house, giving me the perspective of an orchestra pit. She secures her hat when a gust blows, allowing the gown to part, before putting down the book and looping the sash.

Discarding the hat, she moves to the far corner and goes up on her toes for a better view of something, fingertips on the wall, arms giving her lift. The presentation mimics an image at the prow of a ship, and she holds the pose for more than a minute, hair flowing in waves. Turning toward the manor, she walks along the parapet. Her outstretched fingers skim the surface as if in search of engravings. Or maybe she's connecting with tiled images.

Someone or something diverts her attention. She gathers the hat, book, and coffee mug to underscore her exit. Show over.

A mob of shadows mimes chaos on a wall to the left, silhouettes of limbs and leaves from a windblown tree. Yet the projecting sun sheds light on my confines.

I'm pacing the room when recall hits home. "You do know she was acting." That's what Pilar had said about Sarita. Last night she counseled me on the restraint of an "observant man."

Fully woke, I double-check my surroundings for any openings or cracks. There are no loose floorboards, and I find no rusty rods barring the windows. Outside the apartment I yank the padlocked chain on the wrought iron gate, but nothing gives. From the landing, though, I see that Yosef's car is back in the garage space, its barn door open. He must've returned before I woke up.

Preparing for whatever may happen, I resume walking back and forth. *Stay on your toes, Tourneur.* Movement out the corner of my eye alerts me to Yosef coming down the staircase from the manor. He crosses the driveway toward the carriage house.

I revisit the landing. Climbing the steps to the gate, he directs me to back off while he unlocks the chain. Swinging the gate open, he pulls a pistol and gestures for me to follow him as he descends sideways to the parking level.

From his jacket he tosses my wallet onto the hood of his car. Next, he removes my burner phone and places it beside the wallet.

"She convinced him to let you go," Yosef says. "I suggest you make your way to Mérida or Cancún."

Pilar knew her audience, and I'm the beneficiary.

"What's happening?" I say, restarting my search for the big picture, widescreen.

"Don't you know?" he says. "You were pretty cocky last night, thinking you have all the answers."

"What I know is that you felt compelled to kill, to protect us and yourself from dangerous men. Why did they visit PDL?"

"They're no longer here," he says. "So there's nothing for you to worry about. They've come for the daughter of the revolution. Now go."

"Which means what?" I say. "When will you tell Badge Prescott? You realize he's expecting the time and place."

"That's our business, Tourneur," he says, waving the gun at me. "Get moving while you still can."

The only feint at my disposal is to refrain from threats or promised retribution. Not knowing me, he may be fooled. Picking up the wallet and phone, I walk out via the opened garage door.

"Here's one message you can give Prescott," he says. "This week's delivery was his last batch of gyravenal. The doctor will never forgive him for what happened to the shahbanu, his empress."

"I'll tell him to call customer service," I say, raising a thumb to Yosef.

Surprised that I got back the burner phone, my view is that, beyond the gyravenal news, Rashidani wants me to report to Badge the full extent of his wrath over Sarita. Coming from me, the culpable middleman, would add an element of shared guilt to the indictment. And the sooner I do so, the more it would please Rashidani. But it's not a priority for me.

When I reach the main road, I come upon the boy singer and female guitarist encountered yesterday, now playing for commuters and shoppers headed into town. The boy addresses me as "Médico," because of the green scrubs I'm wearing, and offers to sing any song I'd like to hear. Requesting the corrido Pilar and I heard on the bus, titled "Margarita," I submit another generous tip once he finishes and inquire if he'll be there in the evening. "Absolutamente," he says. Making plans on the fly to liberate Pilar requires free association of possibilities. Communication is high on my list of needs.

Local van service returns me to our hotel, two towns away. I change out of the scrubs into jeans and a cotton shirt distressed from the flooded labyrinth in Puerto Rico. Obtaining the manager's recommendation, I connect with a guy who drives me to Brew Peña's archeological site. Once there, a member of her team guides me past a generator toward a platform tent serving as both a conference room and a dining facility, before running off in search of Brew. Seated and hunched over a tabled map of the area, I feel a scratch from inside my shirt pocket. It's a shard of human bone found in the caves three days ago.

Brew joins me at the table a few minutes later, summoned from the depths of a dig. Trust being the watchword of the day, I reveal my true identity—no longer Jamie Boone—then explain the facts of Pilar's captivity and express my goal of freeing her. Brew listens without reacting, drinking some water from a container pulled off her belt. Her silence is a cue to continue.

For context, I sketch the complicity of Pilar's captors in a terrorist plot organized by allies of a non-European nation. Not naming the country, I divulge that it shares with the US a twentieth century history of mutual intervention and trauma. My generality on this point assumes that what Brew doesn't know can't hurt her. The allusion to conflict draws her out, nonetheless.

"During the Cold War, the term 'third world' grew more heads than Hydra," she says. "It pigeonholed countries— possibly including your unidentified nation—that were outside of Soviet Russia and NATO, China and the US."

"Positives like foreign aid were tainted by a crude expression," I say.

"Not just the expression, the intent," she says. "It reeked of condescension. We'll keep you from starving, and you're very lucky we're here."

"Receiving food but not sitting at the same table," I say.

"Worse," she says. "International aid opened doors to violation. Helping to overthrow the democratically elected governments of Iran, Guatemala, and Chile was not seen as a gift, by their citizens or history."

"But since those events are historical truths, we commit to never again."

"Never say never, Senator, when it comes to superior attitudes and the different ways to act out."

"Where do you see it?"

"For me, the most blatant abuse is cultural," she says. "An air of disdain hazes the view of any people whose history isn't Euro derived. Only China and Japan have escaped the arrogance."

"They have some of their own prejudices."

"Sure, but get back to basics. Whether you cite 50,000 years ago, or 100,000 years, so-called modern humans have been around for a long time. A wooden structure found in Africa—notched logs—is over 400,000 years old. It is a fact that many, many peoples developed to a point where stonemasons, carpenters, smiths, botanists, and herbalists contributed to everyday life. Timelines ranged. Some cultures expanded their footprint or migrated due to accidents of location, weather, or natural events, which either empowered or depleted. Emphasis on accidents."

"What doesn't kill me, makes me stronger."

"Not necessarily better," she says. "And not always wiser. The human factor is a wild card. Diversity of thought. Personal aspirations. Emotions eclipsing rationality. The commonality of these variables is what places all cultures on the same plane."

"Mayan and vegan."

"Your words, not mine," she says. "When I was a kid, my grandfather took me to the Cirrus Club for lunch. At the top of the Chrysler Building in New York. The place was filled with lords of the patriarchy. CEOs of airlines and oil and gas, lawyers, ad men, bankers, architects. Grandpa knew them all. I was oblivious, enjoying the view of Manhattan draped in his cape, which he wore over his suit coat in the fall. There I was, ordering chocolate ice cream for dessert and happy as a quahog at high water."

"You just touched on two of my basic needs."

"Go tell the vegans," she says. "After lunch, we went down to the safe deposit vault of Manufacturers Hanover, an old bank, in the Chrysler Building's arcade level. As we were leaving, my grandfather stopped near a woman standing at the door to a boardroom and staring at a painting inside. It was a portrait of Walter Chrysler. Grandpa asked if she needed help. She declined, saying she had worked for Mr. Chrysler long ago and liked to pause by his picture."

"A measure of her honorable and faithful service," I say.

"That's the gist of what my grandfather said to me then," she says. "He added that the strength of relationships—bonds formed through human interaction, my words—is the mark of a professional. I remember that last part because he repeated it in a note when I received my PhD."

"A person alone can only achieve so much," I say.

"That's some of it," she says. "At the same time, you respect choices of those who've earned your trust, even when they differ from your own."

"The wild card."

Brew nods, stretches back, and reaches out to rub the tabletop.

"Given the way you described Pilar's confinement, and what led to it, she may yet devise her own escape," she says. "What's more, you should consider that her choice, which bought your release, may have been affected by disagreement with her bosses, on the one hand, and even deeper regrets over following orders, doing what she was told against her better judgment. Negativity may have festered."

What Brew says resonates. In fact, some of my words and behavior—pursuing Pilar to Mexico against her wishes—put me among the bosses with whom she disagreed. As Yosef said, I was cocky in my demands for information, a bossy cockiness based on a false surety that Badge Prescott controlled Rashidani through a fear of exposure. That is, if and when Badge perceived Rashidani had reneged on their longstanding intel agreement, Badge could lock him up and initiate a government takeover of the entire PDL enterprise. I was misinformed.

While Pilar may be harboring negative feelings—deep regrets over following orders and not pursuing leads sooner—she was far ahead of me in scoping out a sea change in the dynamic between Badge and Rashidani. She intuited that

Rashidani's open anger about Badge's behavior, combined with Badge's playing down the expected intel from Yosef, signaled a shift in the balance of their Faustian pact. Despite that acuity, her actions in saving me may yet have carried an element of self-blame for the fine mess we were in, given the shock of PDL's direct tie to the plot.

Accepting as possible Brew's view of Pilar's mindset, I realize I'll have to coax her for any assistance.

"Helping her escape is a vow she was right," I say. "That could snap her out of it."

"If you fail, you'll ruin what she intended," she says. "An act of duty overturned."

"I don't plan on failing."

"Keeping you alive was the purpose. That's her incentive for staying put."

"Duty's not about one person," I say. "It's what one person can do for others."

"The human factor strikes again."

"I'm trying."

"A wild card," she says.

"De rien."

"Y todo."

"She and I share a calling," I say. "The work goes on, and I can't do it alone."

"What do you need?"

I need input on an escape route—directions, destination, transportation, and passage to the US. Brew advises that taking the main road east to Cancún or west to Mérida would be a mistake because they're the obvious choices. Rashidani would send people in both directions. Heading north to the Gulf coast and paying a fisherman to take us to the Florida Keys is the best alternative. She shows me a map of roads to the Gulf and points out one that ends near a cannery. We could hail a van along that road transporting workers in the hours before dawn. As a precaution, Brew provides a printed layout of the Mayan ruins north of PDL's plant. She briefs me with tips to navigate the grounds should we seek cover there.

Inside a cargo truck where their equipment's stored, I find the rope that I need, including a line with a grappling hook I may be able to use. Brew offers me flashlights, as well. Spotting some straw cowboy hats on a stack of boxes, I ask if I might take one.

"I'll pay for it," I say. "Along with everything else."

"Save your money," she says. "You'll need it for the boat passage."

"I'll pay you later, then."

"Don't worry about it."

"I do worry about it," I say. "Here I am taking equipment from your operation, and you haven't even verified my story. How do you know I'm really a senator?"

"Who'd say they were who wasn't?"

ROPE, HOOK, and flashlights in a canvas bag, I return to the fields next to PDL's plant late in the day. The singer and the girl guitarist are entertaining pickers heading home. Once the audience thins out, I approach them to relocate to the carriage house beside Rashidani's manor, where there'll still be overtime workers leaving the fields on the other way to the road. Offering generous compensation, I explain that I want them to repeatedly perform "Margarita," the ballad of a young man pining for a woman who left him after he gave up everything. My proposal bears a further request—that, throughout the song, the singer inject a brief chorus of "la terraza después medianoche," the terrace after midnight.

The girl, who's the boy's sister, refuses the money, explaining that she has to go home. The boy protests, but she blocks his attempts to claim the cash. I suggest a solution, whereby I'll pay to borrow the guitar for an hour, to be returned to her by her brother. After repeated promises, and a payment hike, she agrees, then shows me how to strum a single chord. I can't handle more at the moment.

The boy and I make our way toward the carriage house, traveling through the grove of trees. We give a northerly wide berth to the courtyard framed by the morgue, medical, and research buildings, and join a thin procession of workers on the way to the road. The door to the garage within the carriage house is shut. Since it's nightfall on Saturday, I'm figuring Yosef is not around.

We stop at a spot facing the manor, and I sit on the ground to warm up, head down, hat tight on forehead, shoulders hunched over the guitar. The boy spreads a red bandana on the grass and puts down some bills, held in place by a few coins. I set a varied rhythm to my strumming, and he begins to sing "Margarita." He gets through at least eight verses, and I haven't heard a single chorus of "la terraza después medianoche," so I start filling his pauses, singing the line myself.

He doesn't take the hint or maybe he forgot or maybe I didn't get my message across. He pares his pauses and crowds my line. First I cut la, then después. Fortunately, between the cadence and his breathing needs, I can still squeeze in terraza medianoche. I tap his leg to interrupt and straighten things out. While we're talking, a woman crosses the driveway from the manor's outside staircase and tosses cash onto the bandana.

"La señorita," she says, pointing up at the house.

Evening's settled in, but peeking from under the hat, I can see that Pilar's not on the terrace, and my scan of lighted windows finds no one. I'm worried she didn't hear enough or wasn't listening closely.

"Momentito," I say, as I snatch the bandana, money spilling out, and pull the bone shard from my pocket, head still down. I fold the bone into the cloth, tie a tight knot without making a show of it, and hand it to the woman. "Para la señorita," I say, tugging the brim of my hat in thanks as she leaves.

The boy and I resume our performance. The go-between's appearance has added lilt to his voice, and the pending contact with Pilar boosts my rendition of "terraza después medianoche." A few farm workers even stop to listen, while I peer beyond them to focus on the house above.

Pilar's silhouette moves on the terrace. There are no torches tonight. Though it's dark out, ambient light from the manor casts a shadow of the boy upon the carriage house. *She can see us*. As we end the song, I lift my strumming hand high after slapping the body of the guitar. We don't hear applause, but I see her hands mime clapping for our duet and take that as a yes. She disappears from the terrace.

The boy gathers the money from the grass, and we head for the road. Approaching town, I stop to return his sister's guitar, pay for the bandana, and reward him for a job well done.

Circling back along the bean field, I walk through the grove toward the carriage house with my loaded canvas bag and come upon a picnic table in a clearing. It's a perfect place to prepare for the task at hand.

CHAPTER 20

There'll be no chimes at midnight, but my burner phone keeps time. It's 11:30 p.m., and I'm climbing to the terrace, coiled rope and grappling hook over my shoulder and flashlights clipped to my belt. An outcrop supporting the terrace rises higher on this southern end, with a number of crags for holds, so I won't have to use the hook to scale the wall. But rope secured by the hook will make for a faster descent. I linked the line already spliced to the hook to a longer length of rope via interlocking loops secured by bowline knots, then tagged the longer rope with grip knots.

The sky is clear and the moon near full. Reaching the terrace, I stay low to avoid shadowing the stars. At the northeast corner, by the house, I unload the rope and hook and start to uncoil the line but freeze upon hearing a vehicle. Doors slam, and voices sound with the tenor of alcohol. Feet hurry up the stairway. I'm thinking Pedro, Rashidani's guard, called over some friends because the old man's gone to bed.

A peep over the terrace parapet confirms two guys being greeted by Pedro and entering the foyer. This should work out well. Pedro will be occupied, freeing Pilar from surveillance. It'll be her call when to make a break for the terrace, whether at midnight or a little later.

I fix the grappling hook in the corner, prongs hard against the joining walls, and run out the rope on the terrace floor, fully uncoiling the connected lines. Sitting with my back to the parapet, I peer at the sky to get a read on the moon and stars. Fleeing in the dark, we want to be sure our heading remains north.

From inside the house, I hear a man's voice, then Pilar's. A bawl of pain is followed by a smash of pottery. I try to open the one entryway off the terrace, a screen door, except it's locked. The upstairs hall is empty, but I pick up a mixed chorus of voices downstairs.

Running back to the front, I see Pilar being chased by a guy down the stairway. Grabbing the rope, I stand on the wall, take a measure of my target, let go slack, and kick off, hands tight above one knot and legs hugging another, then adjusting my swing's trajectory on the fly with foot taps against the bulwark, finally crashing into the guy feet first. Getting up, I'm prepared to take him on, but he's not moving much.

"Senator, you're fully fledged," Pilar says. "Let's go."

I catch up and guide her in the direction of the bean fields. Brew's printed layout of local Mayan ruins shows an ancient causeway, known as a sacbe, running north and south, just to the east of the cultivated land. We reach it and go left, heading toward the coast. After a ten minute run, we come to a clearing. It's a pebble and rubble plaza with patches of grass, surrounded by Mayan stone structures: towers, galleries, colonnades, perimeter walls of a ball court, and a pyramid. Moonlight defines the geometric forms with a rigidity I've only seen in lithographs. From the bottom stairs of a gallery, we spot in the distance behind us the headlights of two vehicles. One turns south on the causeway, while the other follows in our direction.

"Brew told me about an underground passage going north," I say.

"Where is it?" she says.

"The entrance is over there," I say, pointing toward the pyramid, at the far end of the site.

We sprint to the pyramid. An opening under the northside exterior staircase leads to ascending steps in a tunnel, rising over an older, superseded edifice. The walls are cold and moist. I turn on a flashlight and hand the other one to Pilar.

"Wasn't this supposed to be underground?" she says.

"Sometimes you have to rise above to go below," I say. "Counterintuitive as that may be."

"Counterproductive is more like it."

"You'll see."

The tunnel shrinks as we climb, to the point that we're on all fours, and my shoulders rub the walls. Ahead, at the top of the stairs, the flashlight finds a statue of a jaguar. Once reached, the statue's chamber is wide enough to spread arms but not high enough to stand.

Following Brew's instructions, I tilt the stone jaguar forward, raising its slab base to reveal a parallel tunnel underneath. Pilar enters, and I follow, closing the hatch by first lifting the statue upright, then pulling grips notched under the base to slide it over the opening.

We descend facing the steps, as on a ladder, until the tunnel expands to allow walking down face forward. Still later, we find ourselves on a level surface, but one cluttered, and occasionally clogged, with rocks and detritus. Progress would be near impossible without a flashlight, so we shut one off to save the batteries. Right after that I bang my knee on a block of stone.

"Why didn't you all know PDL was involved in the threat?" I say, having cursed to myself rubbing my knee. "You had an embedded agent."

"Those were your words, Senator," Pilar says.

"Turns out they were true, but lacking."

"What do you mean?"

"He's an embedded *double* agent," I say. "Jumping Jehoshaphat, what a surprise."

"For the two of us," she says.

Per my phone, we've been on this level, underground trek for about thirty minutes when we come to the end of the line. We know it's the end because we're confronting a metal door fastened with a padlock. I'm wondering when's the last time Brew traveled this passage. Or maybe she just never knew about the lock.

We're lucky there's plenty of loose stone around because it takes a dozen hammering, slamming, knocking, banging, pounding strikes—using ever larger rocks—to dislodge the hinged clasp secured by the padlock. Turning off the light, we wait a moment to let our eyes adjust, then pull open the door. Outside it's still moon bright. There are three steps up to a path overgrown with foliage. We pass through the brush and find ourselves at a road.

Headlights flash on, facing us, from a pickup truck backed into the woods on the other side. Stunned, I don't move, but hold fast to the notion there's only one person who'd be waiting for us at this spot. A bad guy would've glared high beams. The truck moves onto the road, Brew behind the wheel.

"Are you here to deliver chocolate ice cream?" I say, opening the front door for Pilar, then getting in the back seat.

"It's my turn to play the wild card," Brew says.

"That's what comes from hanging out with the senator," Pilar says.

"You still call him senator?" says Brew. "Honey, hush."

"She says senator and questions me like a reporter."

Brew reveals she's arranged for a pilot friend, Ross Klemmer, to fly us in a seaplane as far as the Dry Tortugas. We just have to get to the coast.

"He owes me," Brew says. "In the short term, that is. Overall, I owe him. But last year Ross got caught up in a theft of antiquities from Honduras. He provided transportation. Didn't know what these men were carrying. The legal authorities thought otherwise. I was his character witness."

"Earned trust from one professional to another," I say.

"Indeed," she says. "We go back a long way. Unfortunately, the authorities weren't as trusting. Their deal was that I had to accompany him on the trip to repatriate the Mayan steles."

"Of course, they trusted you," Pilar says.

"And what did I get for that?" Brew says. "Thirty-six hours without potable water. Returning to the plane, after handing over the steles, a bridge collapsed, and a long detour route left us with nothing to drink."

Something pops. I think maybe a tire, but the truck doesn't swerve or wobble. Another pop. There's a car behind us. A person riding shotgun, with an arm out the window, fires a third shot into the sky.

"They want us to stop," Brew says. "But we're not stopping."

"There's probably guys going in all directions," Pilar says. "North, south, Cancún, Mérida. For reward money."

A bullet shatters the right side rearview mirror.

"It'll be tires next," Brew says. "Hold on."

She slams on the brakes. The pursuit car veers off road, leaving rubber as it does so. Executing a hard left, Brew completes a U-turn and presses the gas pedal to the floor. Within minutes we're back near the Mayan site, our pursuers not far behind.

"The hound's still hunting," I say.

"Have to throw them off the scent," Brew says, hanging a turn where only she sees a road, albeit a bumpy one.

Ahead, the top of the pyramid looms over other structures. Brew veers into the ball court and accelerates between its walls. Then she shuts off the truck's lights as we exit the court and come to a stop, off to the right, out of sight.

Headlight beams bounce around as the pursuit car follows our lead and hurtles into the ball court. Brew now steers the truck from behind a wall in a wide turn, ringing round the court's end zone, and flashes its lights back on, an attraction like the wave of a cape. The pursuit car charges as if it might hit us broadside in speeding to cut off our exit.

It never gets that close, braking too late and falling into the abyss of a cavernous sinkhole, one of the Mayan site's open cenotes.

PILAR FALLS asleep on the plane. I work to stay awake, as company for the pilot, Ross Klemmer, and just to be conscious should anything happen.

A twenty-year veteran of the air force, Ross values ways to contribute, fulfilling himself through project jobs and one-off slots with Brew Peña and others, including explorers, scientists, and documentary filmmakers. Being on teams of specialists striving toward untold objectives suits him fine, over and above the endless pleasure of life in the air. He favors the words swell, professional, and good in underscoring the strength of people he's partnered with or worked for, exceptions aside.

The Dry Tortugas are within the roundtrip range of Ross's seaplane. He touches down near Garden Key, where Fort Jefferson is located, and taxis in close to a beach on the eastern end. We wade ashore carrying blankets and water provided by Brew—as well as Abdul Khan's cellphone, which I'd given her for safekeeping—as the plane takes off. Having about two hours to sunrise, we spread the blankets and go to sleep.

I WAKE to birds chirping, a sun that's escaped dawn, and a missing Pilar. Maybe her leaving was what stirred me. She's at the ocean's edge rinsing a knife. Returning and dropping down on her blanket, she jabs the blade into the sand a couple of times and wipes it clean against a clump of seaweed. She sees me staring.

"Pedro," she says. "He came upstairs and found me dressed to go. I left him alive, but he's still three tacos short of a fiesta."

"Rashidani?" I say.

"He was happy the last time I saw him," she says, looking away.

She uncaps one of our liter bottles and drinks some water, then replaces the cap and carefully plants the bottle in the sand.

"Yesterday at lunch, Rashidani tells me it was Badge Prescott's idea to turn Yosef into an agent," she says. "It's another reason he's pissed at Badge."

"Why is he upset about that?"

"He considered it unnecessary to recruit Yosef and was mortified at having to disclose, in the process, that he was an agent himself."

"From what I've picked up, Yosef was sent over as his eventual successor. Rashidani isn't going to live forever, even with gyravenal. He had to understand the reasoning."

"As you saw the other night, he's proud of his medical discoveries," she says. "He told me he's actively shared them with scientists in Iran."

"Which may have something to do with the men in black visiting PDL."

"Of course, but that's the point," she says. "His ongoing contacts are more valuable than Yosef's. Apparently, the guy did a couple of years in the army but comes from a family that owns factories, including some in Turkey. Yosef is a businessman."

"Fine. Rashidani should reassert his value by telling us all he knows, including the when and where of the attack."

"Once all needs have been met. That's what he said. I wasn't in a position to deliver a comeback. Compromised is a simple way of putting it."

Simple but too little. The weight of it cues me that I've spoken no words of gratitude.

"I owe you my life."

"One of many, Senator," she says, her face skewing quizzical. "You're like Elfego Baca, the legendary man with nine lives."

"Don't know him," I say. "Many parts, maybe, but just one life. I still have it because of how you acted."

She traces a spiral in the sand with a finger.

"I'll give you a shout-out when I get my Oscar," she says. "I'm bringing up Rashidani's complaint to show why I feel dissed by Badge. It's worse than not listening to me. Before I was assigned PDL, he made an entry in the bureau's file calling the turning of Yosef a counterintelligence coup. The whole write-up was a sleight of hand, with masked references to allied and inter-agency sources."

"Why did he do that?"

"That's not straight in my mind yet," she says. "But having read the file entry, I toked the smoke of Yosef as a potent source and treated him with extreme deference. I was duped."

"You were misled by the file."

"I was misled by Badge Prescott," she says. "The first time I came to Mexico to meet Yosef, this major turncoat, I spoke with him about separation pains, shifting loyalties. I was sympatico, admitting my disappointments in the US, times I felt let down by my country. Yet still hoping for positive change. Someday."

"You were building trust."

"Yosef tells me he had a revelation. PDL's medical advances and financial gains were gifts for the betterment of Iran. The threat of losing those gifts—if, at some point, we exposed Rashidani and shut down PDL due to lack of intel—that potential affliction justified his becoming an agent for the US."

"A reasoned remedy."

"More of an overdose. Which is how I felt yesterday when Rashidani told me convincing Yosef to be an informant ended up being easy, once he saw how much the guy liked blondes."

"And so far, no top-secret plans, no arms shipments, no insurgent training camps?"

"The only secret I got from him—before the teaser nods on Imposing Encounter—was during my initial visit. Badge had sent a picture of me to Rashidani, who told Yosef I reminded him of his empress, whom he called Shahbanu."

"Sarita."

"Yosef went on to dish about Shahbanu's exploits and connections," she says. "Knowing Rashidani's predilection was useful, but I never imagined filling the script."

Rashidani's raging over Sarita's death. Badge's tempting, or perhaps taunting, the man with an image of Pilar. It doesn't take long replaying their propensities to see the residue of a triangle. But all that is a sideshow to the feelings voiced by Pilar.

"Besides your issues with Badge Prescott, when have you felt let down by your country?" I say.

"This isn't the time."

"I hear enough of that in the senate," I say. "You've earned the floor."

"When I was in the fifth grade, my father was elected to the San Antonio city council. He had been a precinct chair for Bexar County and was a campaign volunteer for many years before that. The summer of his first year in office, we went for a beach vacation on Padre Island, off Corpus Christi. On the drive home we were stopped by local police. They said our car matched the description of a vehicle used in a robbery."

"That's all they had?"

"It was just an excuse to mess with us," she says. "They told us to get out of the car. My father protested and let them know he was a city council member from San Antonio. They refused to listen, ordering us out and searching the car. When my father tried to keep them from opening suitcases— they opened one, and clothes hit the ground—they cuffed him, and we all went to the police station."

"Did you call a lawyer?"

"We didn't have to. We're there ten minutes when a call came into the station that the actual thieves had been apprehended. After a while, they informed us we were free to go, saying they wouldn't prosecute my father for obstruction."

"No apologies?"

"None. My father felt shame at being cuffed in front of his family. He was incensed by the overall disrespect. I cried every night for days, holding onto his pain and wanting answers."

"Cruelty comes easy for some."

"My father's people—our ancestors—have been in Texas since before 1836."

"The border crossed your people."

"That's the line," she says. "Borders reset, sometimes psychologically. My father served out his term but didn't run again. Since then, he's devoted his free time to performing

Tejano music with friends, retreating to a place where his rights aren't challenged and his gifts are welcomed."

"The voters of San Antonio welcomed him."

"I refresh that memory every father's day, but the bitter root clings tight."

"Once you finish making America safe, you should manage his next run for office. Get him to do it. We need people who don't let their country down."

She raises a hand toward me. I press mine to hers, then she rises.

"Where are you going?" I say.

"Inside the fort, Senator, to the park service office, for assistance," she says. "Could you find out if one of those boats over there at the pier might give us a ride?"

CHAPTER 21

A few boats are docked at slips joined to a pier along the outer wall of a moat surrounding Fort Jefferson, a relic of the Civil War era. On my way to the pier, blankets and water bottles in hand, I pass campers emerging from tents on the beach. Four open boats are empty. Their parties may be among the campers or out exploring the island and its fort.

There's a cabin cruiser, moored stern first, with no one in the cockpit. A shade moves over a porthole. Late sleepers, I guess. Next to the cruiser is a vacant berth for a ferry to Key West. A sign says it arrives at 10:30 a.m. and departs at 5:30 p.m. Another set of signs provides a capsule history of the Dry Tortugas. I finish reading the history as Pilar returns.

"Our friend Ponce de Leon anchored here in 1513," I say. "The absence of fresh water is no fountain of youth."

"It helps in keeping the weight off," she says. "Inside they have a rainwater catchment system and a desalination processor. That's it. Bottled water and all other supplies come by ferry." She eyes the schedule. "We don't want to wait till five-thirty."

"How did it go with the park service?"

"It's just a small staff. But I was able to download and print my bureau ID," she says, holding up an image of her badge in a clear, plastic tag.

"Good morning," says a woman, from the cockpit of the cruiser.

"Good morning," we say.

The woman is wearing a sleeveless cotton blouse over pleated shorts and a visor over a pageboy cut of blonde hair. Her right hand rests on the transom, closed as if clutching a golf ball, while her left lays back, possibly holding a club, but there's no putting mat on the deck. Then I see a coffee mug lying on its side near the helm, as the left arm moves forward, putter in hand. Her appearance is crisp, with sun off the water sharpening her trim form like one of those foamboard cutouts of celebrities.

"Another day in paradise," she says.

"How long have you been here?" Pilar says.

"We arrived yesterday. We're heading back to Key West as soon as my husband has his coffee. He needs to finish another chapter of a book he brought."

"We came in late last night," Pilar says.

"Were you on the plane?" the woman says, and I nod. "I woke up. By the time I got on deck, it was taking off. All that moonlight on the ripples from the pontoons. It turns you on. My husband didn't believe me. He said I was dreaming."

"I'm with the FBI," Pilar says, handing her the ID.

"How about that?" the woman says, examining the badge. "It's a pleasure to meet you, Pilar. Nicole. I'm Nicole Sears."

While Nicole is looking at the badge, I notice that underneath the boat's name on the stern, *Spindrift*, is printed Newport RI.

"We're agents on special assignment," Pilar says, gesturing to me. "My associate..."

"Jamie Boone," I say, realizing she's forgotten my cover. I affect an Irish accent in the hope that, together with a scruffy appearance, I might avoid being recognized by these Rhode Islanders.

"Nate Tourneur," Nicole says.

"Begging your pardon," I say.

"Senator Tourneur," Nicole says. "You look just like him. But I've only seen him on television."

"You've caught me unawares," I say. "What state is he from?"

"Rhode Island," Nicole says. "That's where we live. We retired to Naples for ten months of the year, but we still have a condo in Newport. We haven't been there in a long time. Our grandsons use it. My husband's navy friend has a house in Naples. He and his wife were joining us on this trip. But they fell out."

"Of what?" Pilar says. "The boat?"

"My boss has had a long night," I say, turning to look at Pilar. "Nicole's husband and his navy friend had an argument."

"No, they didn't," Nicole says.

"Just a falling out then," I say. "As you said."

"No, not at all," she says. "I'll tell you who *did* have an argument. Dally Shivern threw a crystal glass that bounced off Charlie Shivern's shoulder and smashed on the tiles as it slid into the pool. Charlie was in the navy with my husband, Bain. Have you ever had to deal with broken glass in a pool?"

"Not in recent memory," I say.

"It can wreck a filtration system. I was thinking of that on the tour of Fort Jefferson yesterday. What if broken glass got into the desalination processor? Talk about diamond crystals."

"That's why I go for spring water," I say, raising a bottle high.

"Bain says the same thing. He doesn't like it here because there's no fresh water. It was my idea. We had some kids from the supermarket load the boat with more than two dozen bottles. Since Charlie Shivern, his friend from the navy, cancelled on us, Bain has to steer the boat all the time. Can't read his book. I said I'd help, but I never got a driver's license, because I grew up in New York City. Except there's no traffic out here. I can steer when there's no traffic. I steer a golf cart with no problem. Bain says if I steer the boat, we might end up in Cancún, even without traffic. Is that so bad?"

"Not a wee bit," I say. "Once the sun is over the yardarm, margaritas are yours for the asking."

"He's okay," Nicole says, looking at Pilar. "Don't lose him. My husband lost Charlie. Who knows what happened?"

"Jamie was in the navy," Pilar says. "Maybe he can help."

"What?" Nicole says. "The Irish have a navy?"

Bain Sears is not overly pleased when he finds that Nicole has invited us to join them on the cruise to Key West. He accepts our company after a fifteen minute chat, wherein Pilar conveys, in general terms, highlights from her career in the FBI, and I provide a summary of my own postings in the navy, under the guise of Jamie Boone, immigrant from Ireland and naturalized citizen.

Once we leave Fort Jefferson and Garden Key and navigate out of the Dry Tortugas, Bain sets a course for our passage to Key West. He and I go back and forth with navy stories, adding commentaries on lessons learned, people commended, and the consequences of actions. Pilar and Nicole are sitting aft in the cockpit, enjoying the sun and carrying on their own nonstop conversation. Periodically, Bain checks his smartphone to see if Wi-Fi is available yet. He doesn't ask me to take the helm, and I don't offer to relieve him, sensing that encouraging him to go below to read his book might, reasonably, raise suspicions.

Nearing Key West and finding he can access the internet, Bain calls Pilar forward to "humor" him by demonstrating her presence on the FBI's website. She directs him to FBI. gov, then rattles off a mix of numbers, letters, and slashes, followed by her name, and, voila, up pops her image and info. Confirmation obtained, Bain offers me the wheel and leaves the deckhouse for the cabin, to finish more chapters of a book featuring quahog pirates.

Nicole and Pilar join me under the hardtop, opting for shade. I learn that Nicole is a big fan of the movie *Titanic*. In fact, there's a *Titanic* link to her visiting Fort Jefferson. She read in an article that casting Gloria Stuart as aged Rose was informed by Stuart's film portrayal—sixty-one years earlier—of the wife of Dr. Samuel Mudd, confined at the fort for his actions after the assassination of President Lincoln. Nicole values Stuart's performances of unbroken love and devotion in the two roles.

"When passion is alive, you put time on your side,"

Nicole says. "Especially when it's slipping away. I bet you do that a lot, Jamie."

"How is it you mean?" I say.

"During your undercover missions. Countdowns to who knows what, and you're under covers."

"Tension rises when the clock's ticking," Pilar says. "Moments are magnified. Minutes carry more thrills than an hour ever could."

"I know it," Nicole says. "It's like when a ten-foot putt hits the spot, and a solid drive is nothing more than a good stretch of your back. You agree, Jamie?"

"You have me at a disadvantage," I say. "Golf is not my game."

"Who's talking about golf? Under covers is the subject. We're all adults here. Under the covers while undercover. Making time."

"Jamie's being modest," Pilar says. "Under covert cover he commanded a conceited courtesan to cower to his power."

"A brief encounter it was."

"Say no more, Jamie," Nicole says, rubbing my arm. "Pilar, I would love to hear those words again."

We leave Nicole and Bain with many thanks after docking in Key West. Pilar contacts the local FBI authorities, calling their emergency number since it's Sunday. Transferred to another line, she arranges a meeting, and we take a cab to the nearby federal court facility that houses the bureau office. We wait outside, as agreed, for Special Agent Bonnie Chung, who arrives in less than fifteen minutes on a bike, a tennis racquet attached to its cargo rack. Entering the building, we go to the FBI office off the lobby. I wait in an anteroom as Pilar follows Agent Chung inside.

Pulling my phone to check the time, a prompt indicates an unread text. It's a message from my lawyer friend, Jack Callahan, detailing results of a nationwide records search on QTS Sustenance LLC. The company was organized and formally established in New York, then applied and was authorized to do business in Louisiana and Puerto Rico, as well. The message cites pertinent addresses, including one in New Orleans.

We had passed a map of the Gulf of Mexico hung on a lobby wall, coming into the building. I go out to the lobby to correlate QTS Sustenance's nearest location, taking care to jam open the FBI office door with a shoe. New Orleans is due north over the Gulf from Mérida, the city just west of Rashidani's manor house and PDL's medical facilities and plant. And there's an international airport in Mérida.

Back in the anteroom, waiting for Pilar, I dwell on her comments about Badge Prescott's role in creating and hyping Yosef as an intelligence source, and its fallout effect on her. The why of that charade remains unknown. Just like Badge's hiding from both of us the direct role of Rashidani in the pending threat. To me, he might cite protocols above my security clearance, or simply argue there was no objective purpose for making me aware of Rashidani's involvement.

But keeping Pilar, the case agent, likewise in the dark is an omission without rationale. Though she downplayed his importance to the plot during Friday night's dinner, that was in service to her performance. In truth, Badge's withholding intel about Rashidani has to sting her as much as the Yosef deception. It's hard not to imagine that the answers to both acts of duplicity are linked.

Pilar emerges from the far reaches of the FBI office carrying a manila envelope. Under her opened jacket there's a holstered pistol.

"I have the forms to take an air marshal's seat on a flight to Washington," she says. "We called TSA."

"That's good," I say. "If I can't get on the same flight, I'll wait for the next one."

"There's a seat for you, too."

"How did you work that out?"

"You're a protected witness," she says. "I can't leave you out of my sight."

Pilar and I stop at a discount store to purchase a zippered canvas bag, into which she transfers the gun. Taking a bus to the Key West airport, we go to the TSA office with the paperwork and our IDs, obtain boarding passes, and bypass the security check. We find open seats in the departure lounge far back from the boarding gate.

"Where did the Irish accent come from?" Pilar says.

"My mother's side, and movies," I say. "But my bag of tricks is nothing compared to Rashidani's. When I first met him, he was a put-upon traveler and persnickety expert on frozen lobsters coming to life."

"He told me that's what hooked him as to possibilities."

"Do you remember how long he said suspended animation lasts?"

"He mentioned that Sarita went under for four hours. Why?"

"QTS Sustenance has a facility in New Orleans, per a text from my friend Jack Callahan. We know PDL's been involved with cadavers, and there's evidence they were active in transplants, possibly through QTS."

"So?"

"When Yosef let us out of the refrigeration lockers, the bodies on tables in the morgue were gone."

"You're thinking they were sent to New Orleans."

"Yes, but not alone," I say. "PDL could've mixed imitations among the cadavers and flown them out of Mérida. The free trade agreement for the US, Mexico, and Canada streamlines commercial shipments via routine documentation and reduced oversight."

"The suspicious six," she says. "But wouldn't they still be breathing."

"Virtually undetectable. A lowered body temperature nearly stops metabolism. In outward appearances, abra-cadaver."

"They get to New Orleans. Then what?"

"Resuscitation and revival at QTS Sustenance," I say. "And on to wherever."

"Wherever's a giant word, almost as big as bendito."

"What does bendito mean?" I say.

"Either a blessing or a lament, in response to joy or pain."

"Speaking of a pain, Yosef did give me a clue," I say. "He said the suspicious six are here for the daughter of the revolution. Wasn't there a feminist academic who famously endorsed Iran's religious restrictions, including wearing a headscarf? That was her nickname, right? Daughter of the revolution."

"Touran Hooshmand, an outspoken critic of the Shah. She wore the hijab in solidarity with the revolution, to reverse the moral decay of his regime. However, she argued that Islamic rules of modesty applied to men, too. That's the feminist part, which isn't given equal attention by the morality police. But what he told you is not much of a clue."

"Hold on to it," I say. "Like New England weather, your assessment may suddenly change."

Our seats on the plane are not together. Before boarding, we discuss possibly going straight to the FBI headquarters, once in Washington, and reporting on all that transpired. Except that it'll be Sunday night of Columbus Day weekend, and the place will be mostly vacant. So instead, Pilar accepts my honor system pledge to meet her there Monday morning, with each of us spending the night in our apartments.

I've finished an airplane snack and a glass of tonic water when my phone rings. It's a call from Mike Levien, my speechwriter, still working from home with FBI protection.

"I didn't anticipate trying to reach you," he says. "But under the circumstances, I knew you'd want to know."

"What circumstances?"

"Vivian Perske. She's okay. She'll recover. She's in the hospital."

"What happened?"

"She was shot, but she's going to be okay," he says. "I found out about it on TV. It happened last night."

"Where was she?"

"At a bus stop near the zoo, on Connecticut Avenue. She was coming from a movie."

"Have you spoken with her?"

"No," he says. "I just got off the phone with Tori Blumenthal. She visited her at the hospital this morning. Tori said the bullet went through Vivian's Tanakh, her Hebrew bible, inside a bag she was clutching. It lodged in her chest but not deep."

That Tanakh belonged to her husband, the late Senator Sam Jacobs. Vivian calls it a perfect commuting companion, conveying something relevant regardless of where you open it. "The dead teach the living," she often says.

"Any witnesses?" I say.

"No. The news anchors speculated a botched robbery."

"Anything missing?"

"The on-site reporter didn't say. Tori told me her bag and the Tanakh are with the police."

"Anything else from Tori?"

"She mentioned how excited Vivian had been on Friday. About something one of the staff dug up from Thomas Breathard's confirmation hearing in February. From his financial disclosure forms. A company he had invested in. Apparently, it's been in the news over health care fraud. Vivian contacted the information officer at SCOTUS for a response."

QTS Sustenance. Vivian succeeded in pursuing a link to my hanging chad of a memory. I requested the search as something of a diversion, and it almost kills her. She's shot with a single bullet, aimed well, and her bag isn't stolen. Those are hardly indications of a botched robbery.

After we land, I fill Pilar in on what happened to Vivian and tell her I want to call Badge Prescott. Without her cellphone, that requires going to Pilar's place in Arlington to retrieve his home number. Along the way I'm able to purchase a change of clothes to match my resolve.

CHAPTER 22

’m waiting for Badge Prescott behind an Ionic column in the interior of the Lincoln Memorial after eleven. A family with four young children are in front of the statue, all gazing up, except for a toddler asleep in his father's embrace. The daughter stifles a yawn, as one of the other boys sits down on the cold stone floor, arms folded. The mother tugs an elbow to lift him up, signaling with a tap on her partner's shoulder that it's time to go. Leaving, they pass a seated woman with long blonde hair drawing on a pad. The wide-eyed frames of her glasses are poised to catch every detail as she sketches Mr. Lincoln.

Badge enters the interior chamber, and I emerge from the shadow of the column. Catching movement, he turns as I approach, gesturing for him to follow me outside. Together we face the Washington Monument, bathed in light, and its inverted image, a glassy spike in the reflecting pool.

"Is there a reason we're here?" Badge says. "Or just the usual politician's penchant for drama?"

"It's a monument to essential truths," I say.

"Quite," he says. "You're about to stun me with a declamation. Make it fast, or I'll insist on reciting the opening lines of Xenophon's *Anabasis*."

"Unfinished work," I say. "The great task remaining."

"That's it?" he says. "I'll give you one word of Greek, exelauno, which means we need to march forth, pronto. Where's Agent Cruz?"

"You should ask your friend, David Rashidani," I say. "Along with some other questions I'd like you to ask him."

Badge lifts his head high, movement chased by an eyebrow. His mouth holds a grimace for three beats.

"Again with the questions, Tourneur," he says. "That's how you get in trouble. And it appears you've gotten Cruz in trouble."

"About that I'm angry, now and then," I say. "But I got in trouble, I got into this thing, because you put my name on the plotters' list of gullible senators."

"You spent too much time in the Caribbean sun. I'm aiding the terrorists?"

"Not directly. They asked Rashidani for input. The crucial thing is he had no fear of approaching you and exposing his close ties to the planned attack."

"What close ties?" he says. "The truth of Rashidani is an open secret among the loose-knit Kharrazi partisans in Puerto Rico. An intermediary came to him with a need, then he contacted me on a hypothetical. So I made suggestions."

"You were worried that someone from the Gang of Eight—fully briefed, unlike me—might have let slip awareness of Imposing Encounter, causing them to call off the attack. Wasn't that your rationale?"

"Maybe yes, maybe no," he says. "It definitely would've exposed our source."

"Stop with the nonsense about protecting an agent," I say. "Rashidani is only a source when it comes to blaming you for Sarita's death."

"A terrible loss. I'd feel the same way if I were him. But he'll come around and provide a detailed warning in due time, as expected."

"You don't show them," I say.

"Show what?"

"Feelings over the loss of Sarita."

"No less than you display guilt."

"I acted with affection. What was your play?"

"Measure for measure, in kind," he says. "A bit of just deserts for Rashidani, with unintended consequences."

"Nor youth nor age, but an after-dinner's sleep, dreaming on both," I say. "Death in a nutshell."

"Trouble with you lawyers, there's always the talk," he says. "It's week-old news."

"What's not old is the direct involvement of Rashidani," I say. "Turns out, he was in Martha's Vineyard last weekend, participating in the sting. And I saw six mysterious men being treated at his facility in Mexico. Your supposed source Yosef considered them killers."

"How did Rashidani respond?"

"As a scientist. He said he laid them down for a procedure. Where they end up is not his department. Stay tuned for further details."

"We shall."

"Good luck with that," I say. "But why aren't you surprised by his direct tie—contradicting your previous statements—and openly shared involvement, when you have the ability to shut down PDL and lock him up?"

"He knows I'll cut him slack, as long as he delivers," he says.

"You did more than cut him slack. You colluded when you could've just told him no."

"What good would that have done? You water a plant to sustain the buds."

"Sustain?" I say. "Facilitate is more like it. Rashidani went to you without fear because he has something on you."

Badge rolls his head as if expunging a crick in the neck. With a younger man, I'd see it as preparing to fight. You can't be sure what will push a person over the edge, young or old.

"Rhetorical jabs don't warrant a response," he says. "Keep pressing, and maybe you'll receive a reaction."

"I thought it had to be Sarita. Rashidani was so vehement in blaming you. But jealousy about a long ago affair the two of you may have had, by itself, wouldn't fuel the rage I experienced."

"Some men project their own form of disloyalty onto others. It disserves everyone in the equation."

"Equation conveys a link," I say. "I'll take that as a yes regarding Sarita. Speaking of disloyalty, consorting with the partner of a foreign undercover agent qualifies. Her death pretty much freed you from the bonds of blackmail, and Rashidani felt outwitted. He was fired up by a loss of advantage over you. One less card to play."

"It's right what they say about senators," he says. "You have too much time on your hands. That is, when you're not fucking the mistress of a man who represents a state sponsor of terrorism."

"You left out 'unknowingly.'"

"To be perfectly clear, in my own case, a personal liaison without damning correlatives doesn't provide much leverage," he says. "If Rashidani or PDL undertook actions against the interests of the United States, I wouldn't hesitate to apprehend and prosecute, regardless of any claims of indiscretion."

"Hats off," I say. "Glad to know you'd do the right thing despite having to forgo the presidential medal of freedom."

"You left out 'temporarily.'"

"Except for something else. Rashidani has another card to play. I figure this other card is what has him so upset with you. Because while it protects him, it can't bring back Sarita and more importantly, to Rashidani, it can't give him back the decades of being under your thumb. Not being able to fully realize his status as a visionary scientist. Instead, it reasserts your presence in his life."

"What fiction did he spin?" Badge says. "Or is it your own invention?"

"When we spoke on Thursday I brought up a company tied to one of PDL's facilities, QTS Sustenance."

"While discussing your middlebrow fixation with financial statements."

"Exactly, I can be a bean counter when only a few are left," I say. "Did you know—you must know, you're an assistant director of the FBI—that Justice Breathard listed QTS Sustenance as an investment on his financial disclosure form? I can't wait to find out who the other investors are."

Resignation appears in Badge's eyes. With each blink he flips a page ahead, cutting short his prepared remarks. The condensed version is light on rebuttal.

"I want you to know that when there are young ones, kids, we look to find children that can benefit from an organ transplant," he says. "We've helped many such cases."

"That's good," I say. "So, unless an investor's grandchild needs a transplant, QTS markets the organs of children to outsiders, adding that income to cadaver sales."

"It's a legitimate business, well capitalized, with increased returns on investment," he says. "Year to year volume continues to rise. That's the dollars. The lives saved are priceless."

"I imagine that members of the QTS LLC have plenty of friends, family, partners, colleagues, and fraternity brothers who require spare parts," I say. "How well do these priceless individuals compensate families of the donors?"

"Think top of the trees, Tourneur. Benefits cascade down."

"The big picture works for me. More people fill the frame."

"Qui transtulit sustinet," he says. "QTS."

"Who transplanted, sustains," I say.

"It comes from deep in the history of New England," he says. "I'm not an overly religious man, but I know it has biblical roots."

"From a psalm that speaks of casting out the heathen," I say. "Using religion to back acts of oppression, like seizing Indian property."

"We possess, and share, exceptional gifts," he says.

"Much of which was stolen. Roger Williams preached that New England colonists made a god out of land, the way the Spanish worshipped gold."

"The original wokester. Diversity, pluralism, equity. Just words in a rant."

"Call it America," I say.

"Not if I can help it."

"Where was the redress to the Native Americans?"

"Redress? Look at their cousins crossing the border. They extract payment in advance, just by getting in."

"Indentured servitude is not reward," I say. "At Thomas Breathard's confirmation hearing another of his investments got the most attention. Brahmin Enterprise Group. A company they own employs migrant children working adult jobs in US factories. OSHA cited the company for dozens of safety violations."

"Supply and demand. No pain, no gain. Bootstraps are a gift. They forge character."

"They produce profits for investors, and character's got nothing to do with it," I say. "Exploiting children and breaking their bodies are crimes."

"Each passing day represents loss. For all of us. We can't be everybody's grandmother."

"Right now I'm fixed on one grandmother who's fighting for her life."

"You set it in motion."

"Things in motion tend to stay in motion," I say. "I'll call you to account."

"All your authority can't create a trail where none exists," he says.

"Vivian Perske's my fuel, and Abdul Khan is the tool."

"Abdul Khan?" he says. "Abdul Khan is like the wind. Never seen, and missing when wanted."

"I don't need him, I have his cellphone," I say, backing away. "We'll find out who his booking agent is."

Badge draws a small pistol from his windbreaker.

"I brought some external force," he says. "Haven't shot in a while, but wherever it strikes, you'll hurt. We're going for a ride."

The blonde sketch artist appears from inside the memorial and walks in our direction, carrying her folded stool and pad under an arm. Badge lowers his pistol and camouflages it in a pocket. She goes by me and closes in on Badge, who shuffles to his right to allow her clear passage down the stone steps. But she stops and raises her free hand, filled with a gun pointed at his chest.

"Slowly, like lava over asphalt, place your weapon on the ground," Pilar says to Badge. He obliges.

In the spread of the memorial's lighting, I notice a park ranger coming up to us from the far side of the steps. He quickens his pace and reaches into his jacket. Sneakers muffle the strides. Sneakers.

I sprint and lunge at him, leaping off the entrance platform as he levels a pistol. Light flashes and a gunshot pops. Crashing onto the guy, he falls backward, as another gun fires. Then I hear a crack, like a half-sawed two-by-four finished off with a stomp. Riding him prone, like I'm sledding, we slide down a few steps. Grabbing around his right hand, I find the gun's not there and roll off to get to my feet. I locate it two steps up and turn the pistol on him but see that his face is frozen. There's blood glistening behind the ears and upon the neck. His eyes don't blink.

Whipping around, I discover Pilar standing over Badge with her pistol. He's seated at the top step clutching his right arm. Rejoining them, I check to see that the burner phone in my jacket, palmed as a mic while speaking to Badge, survived the crash.

"He picked up the gun when you ran," she says. "I dove and backhanded his arm with the stool." Her left hand shakes holding cracked stage glasses. She's already pocketed Badge's gun.

"You're a lucky man, Mr. Prescott," I say. Badge does not respond.

"I got it all," she says, seeing the burner phone in my hand. Having picked up her personal smartphone at the apartment, she recorded my firing line session with Badge. "How did you know about the ranger?"

"They're not on duty this time of night," I say.

I walk down some steps to stand in front of Badge and look him in the eye.

"You'd better hope Rashidani tells you which way the wind's blowing, so we can get ahead of this thing. There's a passel to answer for, regardless."

"When results are in, we'll see," he says.

"Thanks for the skimpy skinny," I say. "You and he must have the same life coach. I think I know her name."

"You knew more than her name."

"I won't let that stop me. By the way, Yosef said Rashidani spiked your last batch of gyravenal to ramp up its toxicity. Your days may be numbered."

He's on his feet when we leave, looking ready to parachute out of a plane, with more to worry about than a bruised arm.

Pilar's car is parked on 18th Street NW near the headquarters of the Daughters of the American Revolution. I'm reminded of the DAR's refusal to allow Marian Anderson to perform in their Constitution Hall, and the resulting effort of Eleanor Roosevelt to arrange a concert on the steps of the Lincoln Memorial. The good ole days.

"Did Yosef really say that about the gyravenal?" Pilar says.

"No. Just that Rashidani's decided to cut off Badge's supply going forward. But it may keep him occupied at an emergency room for a couple of hours."

In any case, we had planned to go on the lam for the night after confronting Badge. Accommodations are awaiting us at a hotel in College Park, Maryland. I'll contact Mick Golden at Homeland Security first thing in the morning.

"What he said—'when results are in'—could refer to an election," she says, driving north.

"Maybe, except the next federal election's a year away."

"I know," she says. "Still, it might've been a subconscious slip, about something related to that."

"You're thinking the plot's political?"

"It's just a guess, like when you said the suspicious six might be spreading a virus."

"Picking that up from Badge's comment would mean he already knows the terrorists' objective."

"Possibly. Or simply their general intentions. It's how he's handled this all along—pretending everything's within a comfort zone—in contrast to what we've learned recently."

"If so, his complicity's crossed another line."

"Not yet," she says. "But imagine he found out the objective. That he learned about the target from Rashidani. A target he could attempt to defend, up to the limit of known parameters."

"While not succeeding," I say.

"Because maybe it's a loss he wouldn't mourn," she says.

That realization is abrupt. We drive a couple of miles without a word, passing the site of President Lincoln's summer cottage, where he escaped the humidity and focused on issues of the war, freedom, and justice. All on his plate, when in today's senate we often can't muster sixty out of a hundred to simply allow a bill to come to vote.

"As much as I dread the event, I worry about the aftermath," she says, breaking the silence. "The who-knows-what aspects of the plot might combine with a tricky coverup to produce plausible deniability. Badge Prescott's blurring to the max could be the final word."

"I won't quit till there's a reckoning," I say. "You just have to keep me alive."

"That's not getting easier."

CHAPTER 23

n my sleep I relive tackling the counterfeit park ranger, hearing the smack of his head. Rapping on the door of my hotel room wakes me up. I get out of bed and open the door the inch allowed by a security fixture. It's Pilar.

"Something's happening in New York," she says as I let her in. "It might be what we've been waiting for."

"What is it?"

"A bunch of people took over the Statue of Liberty."

"Who?" I say through a yawn. "Excuse me."

"You know, the lady standing in the harbor," she says.

"We've been introduced," I say. "Was anyone hurt?"

"I'm not sure, Senator. The reports are sketchy. There may be hostages. We should get there ASAP."

"Whoa," I say, wiping my eyes and skewing priorities for a moment, despite the news flash. "Speaking of formalities, ditch the senator. Go back to Tourneur. Like in Mexico."

"I don't understand."

"At Rashidani's. You called me Tourneur."

"That's when I was punking you. I can't do that now."

Constancy is a virtue. Leave it for another day, I tell myself. It looks like this one has enough conflict already.

"Fine, Agent Cruz," I say. "I have an idea how we can speed up the trip."

A childhood friend, Liam Tyrone, an orthopedic surgeon now living in Severna Park, Maryland, agrees to fly us to northern New Jersey in his plane. Liam went to West Point and Harvard Medical School, then fulfilled his requisite service as an army doctor before starting a private practice in sports medicine.

"I was his first client," Liam says to Pilar, once we're in the air. "And he lost the case. The two of us were training as altar servers, and Father Roux caught me laughing when we had to respond with 'alleluia' at a point in the liturgy. To impress upon me the seriousness of the word, Father told me I'd have to write alleluia on the blackboard two hundred times. Attorney Tourneur, here, argued that that wasn't possible to do because alleluia is an expression, not a word. He ended up receiving the same sentence."

"I stand by my argument," I say. "You can't reduce the ineffable to a single written word. But I won on appeal."

"Who to?" Pilar says. "The pope?"

"Higher," I say. "Sister Mary Jonah. We weren't even halfway through our sentence when she rescued us from the blackboard. She needed help setting up a movie projector."

"For a screening of *The Mission*," Liam says. "She had seen it before but ran it right then for the three of us, even though we watched it again with the whole school the next day."

"Strength of purpose," I say.

"What?" Pilar says.

"That's what she said about the movie. It shows the strength of purpose."

"As many times as I've told the story, I always forget to mention that part," Liam says. "Yet I can still see her, leaning forward in the chair to speak, hands clasped, her face shaded by the veil."

"I made a point of remembering those words because she was always good to me," I say. "Encouraged me beyond all reason."

"And the movie has a downer of an ending," Liam says. "Except that it stays with you in a positive way."

"I agree," Pilar says. "The first time I saw it, I felt it set me on a path. Like a commencement."

"A path toward what?" I say.

"Faith over ideology."

AFTER LIAM gets us to Linden Municipal Airport, we find a cab for a twenty-minute ride to Liberty State Park in Jersey City. Because of the statue seizure, tourist ferry rides from the park to Liberty Island have been cancelled, but the boats are still transporting law enforcement, EMTs, and select media crews to the island. To gain passage, Pilar calls a counterpart from the New York City FBI office, who is on site by the statue. That call and a confirming text to a security detail stationed near the NJ state park pier gets us on a ferry.

Traveling to the island, Pilar fills me in on what she's found online. Per social media postings, a group called Islamic Cultural Force for Free Expression has claimed responsibility for seizing the statue. So far, that name has not prompted recognition by journalists, police or intelligence sources, or any terrorist tracking organizations. The perpetrators have apparently barricaded themselves inside the statue's crown. News reports cite the taking of three or four hostages, but no other details.

Arriving at the island, Pilar seeks out FBI associates for a briefing, giving me her backpack. I go off on my own, not wanting someone with the bureau to cite the presence of a senator on the intelligence committee in a call or text. Nothing good would come from Badge Prescott knowing I'm here.

Much has changed since the first time I visited the Statue of Liberty at age five, while staying with an aunt who had moved to New York. National Park Service staff members no longer live on the island. All remaining housing was essentially destroyed by Hurricane Sandy, and the footprint of those residences is now occupied by a museum and restaurants.

From a police officer I learn that an alert about the terrorist situation went out early. So most of the rangers and all of the restaurant and museum staff cut short their commute. A couple of senior rangers reported for duty, to provide input on the structure of the statue, including its entry points and passageways.

Traveling to the east end of the island, where the statue faces Brooklyn, I stop among news crews parked on a paved walkway at the water's edge. Their cameras are tilted toward the statue's crown. We're two stories below the wall of an eleven-pointed former fort that is the foundation of the statue and its pedestal. Only police in protective gear are within the plaza constructed above the old fort's terreplein.

Staring at the crown's windows, I can detect movement but no specific details. Those windows are about three hundred feet from where I'm standing. Two helicopters hover in place out over the water, to the right and left of the crown. Beyond having firepower, I imagine those on board are equipped with telephoto lenses to observe what's happening inside.

I walk toward Pilar, who's approaching me from the command center set up by the FBI, the US Park Police, and the NYPD's Emergency Service Unit.

"They took four hostages," she says.

"How?"

"Last night, about 4:00 a.m., sensors picked up a vessel moving within the exclusion zone that surrounds the island. A patrol boat went out to investigate. They had live access to CCTV coverage at the base of the statue. Three young men were carousing around a cooler, like drunken college kids."

"Just three?"

"They only saw three. Plus a boat at the dock. But before docking, the attackers had motored in by the wooded area and unloaded a dozen others, who were armed. After the park police got there and confronted the three, the men with guns emerged from the woods and came up on them from behind."

"That's the type of maneuver well-trained commandos could've executed easily," I say. "Possibly, our suspicious six."

"True," she says. "But a group of well-trained radicals could do the same. It's not hard to acquire a bunch of guns."

"How did they get into the base, the pedestal?"

"They had to break open two doors," she says. "Locksmith tools would've been enough."

"They didn't need explosives?"

"Not for what they've done so far," she says. "And here's the thing. Six commandos would've been able to pull this off, blow up the statue, and escape. What are these people up to?"

At this point she's right. A professional operative could've infiltrated activist groups, recruited extreme members, trained them, and provided money for necessary equipment. There'd be no need to organize an intricate scheme to sneak six commandos into the US.

"Tell me something," I say. "You saw most of the intelligence that Josh Kuhn and the CIA gathered about the security threat. Correct?"

"I saw a lot of raw data and all the reports and recommendations circulated outside the agency."

"Aside from Badge Prescott's deception concerning Rashidani, you found the intel and conclusions credible."

"Absolutely."

"That said, the timing of this is spot on," I say, pointing at the statue.

From atop the parapet of the old fort wall, a SWAT-equipped ESU officer turns and waves an arm toward the command center.

"They've breached the windows," he says.

Arms are poking through open windows in the crown. A man is climbing out of the window above Lady Liberty's right ear. He secures a line over the nearest of the seven spikes flaring out from the crown. Pilar puts her hand on my shoulder.

"Online there's a live view from a permanent camera in the torch," she says, raising her phone for me to see the high angle close-up shot.

A few horizontal casement windows have been removed. Glass panes appear to have been cut from others. The first man out has climbed to the top of Lady Liberty's head. He's tied a line around another spike, with both spike lines attached to a harness strapped to his torso. A second man emerges above the right ear and joins the first, repeating the routine of lines lashed to spikes and fastened to a harness. Each of them sits down, pulls more rope from a backpack, ties an additional line to his harness, and drops that line over the edge of the crown, just to the right of the center spike. The ends dangle in front of the middle windows.

Accomplices inside use mooring hooks to latch onto and retrieve the dangling lines, as the two climbers hammer snubbing winches, together with footholds, into Lady Liberty's hair. Once that's done, they loop their ends of the lines to the winches. Minutes later a mass of black cloth, rolled tight like a fine rug, is pushed through a window, bound upside and back by the two lines running to the climbers.

On an unheard signal, the climbers begin hoisting the lines in tandem, resting between a series of heave-hos, the rope remaining secure around the winches. They lift the roll of cloth to the top of the head and unfurl it, draping a larger portion down to the nape. This portion has long lines attached, right and left, like wraparound apron strings. The two men retain a grip on these apron strings and pass them down to others at the corner side windows, who pull them right-to-left and left-to-right, respectively, keeping the lines outside the window frames as they tug. Lifting and joining the two sides at the middle, they drop the gathered cloth to settle below Lady Liberty's chin.

The front part of the material on top is cut in seven places, so it can pass by the spikes and flow over the crown. The sliced sections resemble tear off pieces at the bottom of flyers put up by people seeking opportunities, missing pets, or lost keepsakes. Accomplices at the windows thread rope through previously hemmed edges of the sliced sections, as the two climbers descend and get back inside. They tighten the belt within those hemmed sections, then let the material fall over the ears and across the forehead, covering the windows in the crown.

There she is, Lady Liberty. In a black hijab but still standing.

"Call it a wrap," I say.

"Where's the party? I'll go see if there's any word about the next step."

I walk with her to the command center but stay outside, holding her backpack, mine over my shoulder. There are smiles on the faces of the news crews and relief in the eyes of law enforcement personnel. Odds that the hostages will be okay have taken a giant leap.

Yet many questions need to be answered. Who organized this brazen attack? Who funded it? Are any foreign nationals involved? And, of course, I remain concerned about the six suspicious men we saw at PDL's facility in Mexico.

Pilar emerges from a throng encircling the command center canopy.

"The Islamic group says they'll start negotiations for release of the hostages in an hour," she says.

"They're probably celebrating."

"Sure," she says. "On their phones or posting or sending out texts telling people to check out the online view from the torch. It's having their cake and eating it, too."

"I've been thinking. What if this statue event was a stalking horse for Imposing Encounter?"

"How?"

"Rashidani's shared science on suspended animation gets in the hands of some Kharrazi people who want to sneak commandos into the US," I say. "He's approached and determines that for what they want, deep sedation would be enough. No need for his advanced procedures. But there's still a hitch."

"What's the problem?"

"They have to use QTS in New Orleans for delivery and revival, along with a regular shipment of real cadavers," I say.

"He needs Badge Prescott to clear the way and limit questions at the QTS facility," she says.

"In exchange for that cooperation, Rashidani offers to provide Badge with intel."

"Badge melds the bare bones of what Rashidani tells him with broader intel, including chatter surveillance on what became the statue seizure," she says.

"That mix of information will add to the ball of confusion he tries to create after our six commandos do their thing," I say. "Of course, he totally holds back the involvement of QTS."

"I could use some café," she says. "It'll calm me down."

"The restaurants are closed."

"One of the tourist boats has a snack bar."

We go down by the docks and board the *Hercules Mulligan*. Finding seats, I leave the backpacks with Pilar and get in line at the food counter. A local radio station is playing through the announcement speakers. I hear "Islands in the

Stream" and "Shattered" before reaching my destination to the sound of "The Ties That Bind."

I deliver Pilar her café and sit down with a bottle of cranberry juice. She's watching a news program on a TV mounted at the front of the seating area. The sound is off but subtitles are transcribing the words of the reporter, who shares the screen with split images of New York Governor Quentin Andreotti and Speaker of the House Desideria Armendáriz-Román.

"Touran Hooshmand wouldn't like this guy," Pilar says.

"Who?"

"Governor Andreotti," she says.

"I know," I say. "Who's Touran?"

"Touran Hooshmand, Iran's daughter of the revolution. She said rules of modesty should apply to men, too. The governor talks a good game, but he has busy hands around women."

"Was the story about next year's presidential primaries?" I say, as the program breaks for a commercial. "They're the leading candidates."

"No, it wasn't about that."

"How was Desi involved?"

"Who?"

"The speaker of the house."

"Oh, DAR," she says. "The governor and DAR are speaking at Grand Central Station in a while. Something about new train lines opening up."

I spring to my feet and seize the backpacks.

"We have to go," I say.

"What's happening?"

"The six commandos didn't come *on behalf of* Touran Hooshmand. They're coming *for* DAR."

"Ay, bendito."

Exiting the *Hercules Mulligan*, I see NYPD patrol boats docked at the far end of the pier, almost out of sight, astern of two other ferries.

"I'll try to get a message through to the police at Grand Central," Pilar says.

"You can try on the way, in the boat," I say, running.

"What boat?"

"One of those," I say, pointing ahead at the patrol boats. "We'll be at Forty-Second Street in ten minutes. There's nothing to it."

choose the lightest boat and open it up to full throttle. Seeking the quietest spot to make a call, Pilar huddles down on the sole, the floor of the cockpit, forward and under the buffer of the windshield.

In a few minutes we've passed the South Street Seaport and are approaching the Brooklyn Bridge. Pilar gets up from the sole to sit by me at the helm.

"I contacted the FBI team," she says, raising her voice to compete with the engines, water under the bow, and spray. "Told them we took a boat and why. They tried reaching Grand Central, but lines are backed up with calls about the statue. They left voicemail messages and will follow up later."

"That's why we're delivering our message in person."

"This is all just your take on a slight but freaky matchup. We don't know anything for sure."

"Not true," I say. "I know that I'm right. For sure. From small things big things come."

"But, Senator, I bet with lots of the crowds you've spoken to, there were threats made in advance. How many turned out to be credible?"

"Zero, and so far they've mostly been anonymous," I say. "With this situation, though, we have plausible intel, and not from an anonymous source. What's more, in an auditorium the crowd's usually gone through metal detectors. At Grand Central, people can come in off the street or up from the subway unchecked."

I glance over, sensing a stare in the absence of a response. Her eyes are tense.

"I won't mind being proven wrong," I say with a smile. "That's the beauty of a six-year term. When it's time to vote, people don't remember half of what you've said or done."

"Recap what led to your epiphany," she says. "Beyond Yosef's comment."

"Start with the timing. In acts of terrorism intention is everything. They don't count on coincidence. Synchronicity only serves the defense. Through quirks that alert."

"The hijab on the statue is a diversion," she says.

"Not just that, but the day itself is a signal. A blow from the global south against colonialism on the holiday of its point man."

"Columbus."

"Outside of an Englishman, how better to highlight the intent than going after an Italian American and a Hispanic American?"

"DAR's a Latina. We carry indigenous blood."

"Doesn't matter. To the wider world the names Andreotti and Armendáriz-Román are European."

"Birthplace of the oppressor."

"Then there's the fact that DAR is a charismatic leader to so many, just as General Kharrazi was beloved in Iran."

"An eye for an eye," she says.

"Speaking of strict moral codes, DAR is against those that subjugate women and deny them agency. How are such advocates treated in Iran?"

"Sent to prisons, where they occasionally turn up dead, or arrested during acts of civil disobedience, sometimes dying in the process," she says, slowing her cadence and lowering her voice.

We overtake a boat full of tourists circumnavigating the island of Manhattan. I turn on the siren for bunches of kids waving at the rails, and the tour boat sounds its horn. Pilar reaches out and grips the control console and leans against me.

"Tourneur, you're good at finding color in a black and white photograph," she says. "You have to keep doing that."

Glints of concern spark narrowed eyes, but the look holds steady. The feeling I observe is beyond duty.

"Everything's going to be okay, Pilar."

"How do you know?"

"Whatever's happening behind your eyes will make it so."

We've reached New Wave Pier, near Forty-Second Street and the United Nations headquarters. I hang fenders and hitch the boat to a stanchion. Pilar's taken two guns from her backpack, giving me the fake ranger's and keeping Badge's to brace with the holstered Key West pistol. We leave our bags behind.

A cab takes us west. Hitting a red light, we jump out at the Chrysler Building and jaywalk Lexington with zeal, dodging e-bikes leading a charge of traffic down the avenue. Music as distant thunder greets us rushing through Grand Central's marketplace passageway. Loaves and muffins and grains and flowers filter the surround sound into pulsating rhythms, but synthesizer notes command the space as we reach the main concourse. Functioning today as something of a concert hall, the atrium's white marble glows under accent lighting, its gold leaf trim and brass fixtures adding to the brilliance.

Dancers are performing on four catwalks within the three majestic windows that open up Grand Central's west end. Strobe lights frame the dance concert with pops of color. Those colors pierce mists of sun overflowing half-moon windows along the south ceiling.

While we scan the atrium for trouble, the dancers move across the windows on skates, scooters, skateboards, unicycles, bikes, and tricycles. Others push-pull grocery carts, strollers, luggage, hand trucks, baggage trolleys, and little wagons. Returning without props, they dance a series of combinations, in solos, duets, and ensembles.

Pilar goes to brief the speaker's and governor's security details on the perceived threat, and I proceed to scout the concourse and balconies. The Statue of Liberty seizure, combined with the holiday and its parade, have taken the "Grand Central Station" out of Grand Central Station. Most of New York City is in front of a television right now.

There are pockets of individuals in the main concourse waiting next to suitcases, and others milling around with campaign signs or joining bands of supporters in candidate tee shirts. But there's no simultaneous movement of thousands of people racewalking to work or an appointment or to catch a train, their myriad intersecting paths weaving a human carpet of contention for right of way. And there's not one person standing by the information booth and its four-faced clock.

The lobby off Vanderbilt Avenue has been cordoned with a single detail of police, detouring incoming transients. As I recon the west balcony—its restaurant completely empty, prenoon—the dancing and music and strobe lights cease. Immediately, Speaker Armendáriz-Román and Governor Andreotti appear, adding volume to the concluding applause for the performance. Using the middle landing of the split west staircase as a microphoned platform, under the three large windows, they face a small crowd of partisan posses, committed constituents, and serious seekers, gathered between the stairs and the clock.

I'm glad the speaker and the governor have come out together, indicating that neither will address the crowd for long. Resuming my patrol, I move toward the north balcony and catch fragments of DAR's comments as I range.

"We celebrate greater access to Amtrak, Metro-North, and the Long Island Railroad, new lines connecting people to opportunities and introducing them to other individuals, shared rides conserving energy and multiplying potential," DAR says, with the governor hanging back, giving her space.

A child in the audience, holding the hand of a woman, points up to the blue ceiling, with its celestial images of stars and constellations.

"Look," he says, filling a pause in DAR's speech with a shout. "There's Pegasus."

Giving a thumbs up to the kid, amidst laughter all around, DAR says, "Education in action is right there in that boy. Learning from the past is key to the future of our world."

Pilar's positioned like a sentry by the information booth and clock in the center of the concourse. She pivots side to side, as she surveys the atrium. Looking down from the north balcony, I catch her eye and draw a stealth nod.

"We channel the concern of individual citizens, you and me, to produce action for those in need," DAR says. "The measure of our lives is in that struggle."

Standing at the balcony near escalators to and from the MetLife Building, I notice people on the catwalks in the center west window looking down behind the landing where DAR is speaking.

"Democracy allows us to truly live our lives in keeping with the sure wisdom of conscience," she says.

There are two men each on a couple of the catwalks. All four are carrying what look to be golf bags. The bags remind me of the many transport devices used in the dance piece. But the show is over.

I dash to the escalator, vault a divider, land on the moving stairs, and scramble down. Exiting into the concourse, I see the four men in the window kneeling and affixing something to the panes of their respective spaces. Sprinting to my right, skirting the crowd, I reach and hurtle up the staircase, taking two steps at a time and yelling with empty hands held wide.

"Get down, everybody down," I say, as windows explode, showering the west end of the atrium with shards and bits of glass.

I hear the first gunshots as I throw myself at DAR on the landing and together we hit the floor. She punches me with fury, then claws at my face like a tiger.

"Desi, it's Nate Tourneur," I say, pulling her out of the line of fire, down the steps on the other side of the split staircase.

Mid the explosive racket, ricocheted bullets and direct hits pit and chip the marble balustrades around us.

"Nate?" she says. "This is some recess."

"Another day on the job," I say, removing the pistol from a pocket. "Like what you said about making the world safe for diversity. Remember what you said?"

"I like it like that?"

"No. It begins at home."

"Be careful," she says.

"Stay down," says I.

Most of the crowd ran when the windows shattered and the blitz began. Others slid off on their stomachs or crawled away, managing to get behind the barrier of the information booth or escaping altogether.

Taking aim from the staircase corner, I select one of the four who are firing assault rifles and shoot for his head, figuring he's wearing body armor. He collapses, either from my shots or those of other guns—police and security—in tandem.

The fusillade continues, as three remain standing, like toy soldiers on shelves in a glass highboy. Concentrated fire seems to lift one of them off his feet, jigging from the catwalk and falling to his death.

Targeting another, I hear Pilar's voice—"Tourneur!"—and a jolt knocks my right shoulder forward, the pistol dropping and bouncing on the marble.

I pick up the gun using my left hand and see Pilar, hands filled with Badge's weapon and her own. She's blazing away at two other hitmen, numbers five and six, who are shooting pistols on the run along the north balcony, behind and above me.

"You're bleeding," DAR says, low and tight against the staircase wall.

Desi can't see Pilar or the jam she's in. Hunched down, she's firing with arms extended and raised and crossing the concourse space like a linebacker tracking a quarterback. While shooting, she has to hop over the few people remaining prone on the floor. She left the relative safety of the info booth to make herself a target, to draw flanking fire away from me and DAR. But she can't neutralize the two hitmen on her own.

To give her cover, I support my left hand on a balustrade and shoot repeatedly, forcing one and then the other hitman to duck for a second or two. I can't tell if either is hit.

Badge's pistol runs out of bullets. Pilar tosses it and bolts for the staircase, still firing her other gun. The two hitmen crouch behind balusters and send bullets flying through what, at my angle, are barely arrow slits between the posts.

After shooting at them again, I come up empty and let go the gun just as Pilar jumps and lands one foot on a brass banister, bounding off that foot for another leap.

I bend over the balustrade, reach out with my left hand, and grab hers. As she dangles in my grip, our eyes fuse, dialing down the din of the firefight around us.

"I've got you," I say.

"Okay, then," she says.

THE SPEAKER and the governor survive the assassination attempt. The governor, however, suffers gunshot wounds, leaving him with severe damage to a leg. That much I know. He'll likely require the use of a cane.

Four of the six hitmen are killed, the other two captured alive when their bullets run out. The captives give no details about themselves or the genesis and mechanics of the plot. Face recognition databases and circulated photographs yield facts of their identities but, early on, little else. They are silent in response to questions about PDL Biopharma and QTS Sustenance.

Supported by my hospital bed deposition, an indictment is obtained against David Rashidani. Evidence includes autopsies of the deceased hitmen, records of a cadaver shipment from Mérida to New Orleans the Friday evening before Columbus Day, and sworn testimony by personnel of QTS Sustenance in New Orleans. Rashidani's appeal of extradition from Mexico is pending.

Badge Prescott retires to have more time with his family and grandchildren. The maneuver won't shield him from scrutiny once national security redactions allow release of FBI and CIA files on Rashidani and PDL. Further tracking of linked activity will expose and magnify the criminality of the QTS shenanigans. Hopefully, years of taking gyravenal revitalized Badge to face numerous counts of indictment in this life and, when he finally dies, the ongoing condemnation of history.

It isn't a priority, with all that's happened, but I find myself imagining another used knockabout. By and by, a proper sailboat presents itself, in the way visions sometimes come to pass. I christen it *Resolution II*.

Now at the helm in a light breeze, I'm using the mainsail

by itself, a single sail. With the first puffs of a wind change, I maneuver the boat about, heading northward.

Southwest gusts warrant raising the jib. I tie down the tiller and go forward, leaving the mainsheet fixed in a cam cleat. Kneeling on the starboard deck, I'm hoisting the jib halyard when the hatch to the cabin slides open, and Pilar's hand pops up.

I lean over, to peer into eyes that hold so much feeling, without fail.

"I'm your partner," she says. "I'll do my part."

Like I don't know.

I grip her hand and give her a lift as she climbs. Momentum carries Pilar's body across mine. I let go the halyard to embrace her and keep her from rolling into the sea. The jib falls, and its sailcloth drapes over the two of us.

Author Bio

Diego Kent is the author of the novel *Rio Los Angeles*. His writing has appeared in *The New York Times Magazine* and *The New York Observer*. His work has been featured at the Canadian International Annual Film Festival and The New York International Fringe Festival.

Made in United States
North Haven, CT
02 September 2024

56434202R00157